The mystery of B[...]

He'd unravel it, no matter how long it took. And this was the first step.

But when he opened her door, her head whipped around to reveal a look of panic.

"You took ten years off my life," she said. "What are you doing here this time of night?"

"I saw the light. Is everything okay?"

"So you've come to save the damsel in distress? My hero." She fluttered her hands. "Or is this just another flirtation from Drew Kinley? I've heard all about you, you know."

"You're smart enough to make up your own mind about lots of things. Including me."

"That's a line."

"No, it's not." He edged closer. "Who was he, Bekah? The guy who scares you so much, you can't trust me not to hurt you the way he did."

Panic seized her features again, but Drew rested a comforting hand on hers. "You can be honest with me."

Bekah had called him her hero. He had every intention of proving to her that he was worthy of that title.

Mia Ross loves great stories. She enjoys reading about fascinating people, long-ago times and exotic places. But only for a little while, because her reality is pretty sweet. Married to her college sweetheart, she's the proud mom of two amazing kids, whose schedules keep her hopping. Busy as she is, she can't imagine trading her life for anyone else's—and she has a pretty good imagination. You can visit her online at miaross.com.

Books by Mia Ross

Love Inspired

Oaks Crossing

Her Small-Town Cowboy
Rescued by the Farmer

Barrett's Mill

Blue Ridge Reunion
Sugar Plum Season
Finding His Way Home
Loving the Country Boy

Holiday Harbor

Rocky Coast Romance
Jingle Bell Romance
Seaside Romance

Hometown Family
Circle of Family
A Gift of Family
A Place for Family

Rescued
by the Farmer

Mia Ross

HARLEQUIN® LOVE INSPIRED®

Recycling programs
for this product may
not exist in your area.

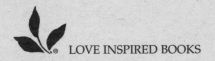

® LOVE INSPIRED BOOKS

ISBN-13: 978-0-373-71966-2

Rescued by the Farmer

www.Harlequin.com

Printed in U.S.A.

Do unto others as you would have them do unto you.
—*Luke* 6:31

For Misty

Acknowledgments

I'm grateful to the very talented folks who help
me make my books everything they can be:
Melissa Endlich and the dedicated staff
at Love Inspired.

More thanks to the gang at Seekerville
(www.seekerville.net), a great place to
hang out with readers—and writers.

I've been blessed with a wonderful network of
supportive, encouraging family and friends.
You inspire me every day!

Chapter One

Okay, it was official. She was lost.

Sighing in frustration, Bekah Holloway squinted through the branches alongside the isolated country road she was currently on, hunting for a sign to tell her where she was. It was probably intended to be two lanes, she complained silently, but considering the washed-out sections and complete lack of a shoulder, it was more like a lane and a half. That made it tough for someone who had no clue where she was going to keep the small hatchback out of the wide ditches on either side.

It sure was pretty out here, though, she had to admit as she drove beneath massive oak trees whose leaves were in the midst of changing colors for fall. It was almost October, and some were still green, but most had gone over to various shades of gold and red, giving her the impression that she was driving beneath nature's own archway.

And it was so quiet, she could actually hear her own breathing. She couldn't recall the last time she'd been able to do that, and she drank in her peaceful surroundings with sincere gratitude. It was a far cry from the traffic jams and crammed sidewalks she'd left behind her less than a month ago. Breaking away from the only life she'd ever known had taken a huge effort on her part, but now that she'd managed to gain her freedom, she'd rather die than go back to her old ways.

That thought had just flitted through her mind when something hit the windshield with a force that jerked her back to reality with a startled yelp. Before her eyes, the already chipped upper right corner of the glass spider-webbed into a large crack. She let out a dejected sigh. Repairing the radiator a few days ago had taken the last of her meager cash. There was no way she could do anything more until she found herself a job.

A fluttering at the side of the road dragged her attention away from her pity party, and she realized that whatever she'd hit was still alive. She wasn't exactly a nature girl, so she wasn't sure what to do, but she couldn't leave an injured animal alone and helpless in the woods, suffering until it finally died. Moving slowly to avoid scaring it any further, she eased the driver's door open and crept to the edge of the gravel lane. There, in a wallow filled with mud, lay the most incredible creature she'd ever seen.

A hawk with striking white-and-rust-colored feathers lay on the ground, clearly stunned but still conscious enough to watch her through one dark, mistrustful eye. The other was half closed, and from the odd angle at which its wing rested, Bekah assumed it was broken. The poor thing was breathing so fast, she couldn't have kept up without hyperventilating. It seemed to her that it was waiting for her to finish the job her windshield had started.

"Please, don't be scared," she cooed to the terrified bird. "I want to help you."

When she moved closer, it began flapping its good wing in a panicky gesture that made Bekah instinctively stop in her tracks. She wanted to help, but she didn't know how.

"Hey there," a deep voice murmured. "Need a hand?"

Terrified by the unexpected sound, she whipped around to find a tall man behind her. Dressed in running attire, he was obviously out for a jog, which explained why she hadn't heard him coming. Apparently, he sensed her fear, because he held his hand out to her with a friendly grin. "Drew Kinley."

Shocked into silence, at first she couldn't make herself respond. He patiently kept his hand within her reach until she managed to reply. "Bekah."

She didn't shake his hand, and out of habit, she stopped short of adding her last name. Either he didn't notice, or he didn't care, because he skirted around her and assessed the injured animal from a safe distance. "Looks bad. What happened?"

"I'm not sure. One minute, I was driving along trying to figure out where I am, and the next, blam! I ran into this poor hawk. I feel terrible," she added in a near whisper. She'd had enough pain inflicted on her in her life to know how it felt, and she knew all too well that being all alone only made the problem worse. Knowing she'd caused this beautiful creature so much pain made her nauseous.

Unfortunately, her confession brought Drew's gaze back to her. His light brown hair was damp from his run, and it occurred to her that his eyes were a unique blend of green and gold she'd never seen before. When they focused on her, she watched as idle curiosity shifted to concern. "Are you okay?"

"Yes." When she realized he was staring at her cheek, she lifted her palm to cover the healing bruise. "This happened a while ago."

Darkening like thunderclouds, those eyes took on a fierce quality that made her backpedal in self-defense. When he noticed her motion, he put on a smile that looked forced but much less menacing.

"I'm sorry, Bekah," he told her in a soothing Kentucky drawl. "I didn't mean to frighten you. I just hate seeing a woman hurt that way is all."

Why did he even care? she wondered. She was a complete stranger, and he'd interrupted his morning run to help her. This sort of innate kindness was so far beyond her experience, she didn't know what to say.

After waiting several seconds, he seemed to understand she wasn't going to respond. "So, back to your friend here," he said in a chipper tone. Unzipping his hoodie, he asked, "Do you have a box for us to put this hawk in to keep him from struggling?"

"You can tell he's male from way over here?"

Looking a little puzzled, Drew shrugged. "Not really. I just assumed."

Typical guy, she huffed silently. "What's wrong with assuming she's female?"

"Good point," he conceded with a sheepish grin. "Do you have a box to put *her* in?"

"Um, no. But I have a big duffel bag."

"That'll do. Why don't you empty it out, and I'll try not to scare the poor thing any more than we have to."

Relieved to finally have a plan, she opened the rear hatch and took out the bag holding all her clothes. She dumped them on the floor of the car and offered the bag to Drew.

Cocking his head, he gave her a half-grin. "Yeah, that's not gonna work. I'm gonna have my hands full of angry hawk, so you'll need to hold the bag for me to drop her into."

Backing away, she shook her head in protest. "I don't think so."

"I can't do this by myself," he reasoned. "There's an animal rescue center not far from here, but I need your help to get her there. Otherwise, I could end up hurting her worse."

That did it for her. Feeling responsible for the poor animal being wounded in the first place, Bekah knew that the least she could do was help Drew get her to someone who could care for her properly. Screwing up the tiny bit of courage she still had in her, she grasped both edges of the bag and followed him to where the bird lay.

"Now, I'll cover her with my sweatshirt to keep her from going nuts. Once her eyes are blocked, she should settle down some, and you can catch her in the bag." Giving Bekah a bracing look, he asked, "Ready?"

"As I'll ever be."

"Good. I'll make sure to get a solid hold on her, so she won't hurt you."

That he was concerned about her safety touched Bekah in a way so unexpected, she didn't know how to process the emotion. In the few minutes she'd known this tall, good-looking man, he'd rattled her thoroughly more than once. And not in the bad way she'd grown so accustomed to.

Yanking her errant thoughts back to the matter at hand, she waited while he spoke reassuringly to the bird, edging closer when she calmed and pausing when she seemed to be growing unnerved by his presence. Finally, he was close enough to wrap the hawk in his jacket, and Bekah stepped up with the duffel bag to enclose the frightened animal.

Cradling the bundle, she felt the bird's frantic heartbeat as if it were her own. She knew how it was to feel powerless, and she cuddled the hawk to her chest hoping to make her feel safer. "It's all right, baby—you're safe now. We won't let any more bad things happen to you."

The struggling eased a bit, and Drew opened the passenger door for her. When she understood what he was suggesting, she took a large step back. "What are you doing?"

"You've got her calmed down, so I figured I'd drive us to the rescue center. Is that okay?"

Not in a million years.

She was more or less comfortable with holding their patient, but the idea of allowing someone else to drive her to an unknown destination filled her with a terror so deep, it was threatening to choke her. That kind of blind trust had caused her no end of trouble in the past, and she wasn't keen to set herself up for that again.

Then logic kicked in to remind her that it would be impossible for her to drive while holding the injured bird. Not to mention, she had no idea how to get to this rescue center he'd referred to. So, undone by necessity, she let out a quiet sigh and nodded. "I guess."

Once she was settled in the passenger seat, he quietly shut the door and hurried around the front to get behind the wheel and start the engine. He pulled his cell phone from a cargo pocket on his shorts and put it on speaker before pulling onto the road. A pleasant voice on the other end answered, "Oaks Crossing Rescue Center. This is Sierra, how can I help you?"

"Hey, it's Drew. I'm coming in with a badly injured red-tailed hawk. Thought you'd like a heads-up."

"Get it here as fast as you can," the woman replied in a crisp, efficient tone laced with concern. "I'll be waiting."

Drew tapped the screen to shut off his phone and tucked it back in his pocket before glancing over at Bekah. "How're you ladies doing over there?"

"Still breathing." Bekah peeked into the bag to check on their passenger. The hawk was coiled like a spring, but at least she'd stopped wriggling and trying to get loose. Either she was calming down, or she was fading fast. Since she knew next to nothing about birds, Bekah realized she had no choice but to hope for the best. "She's really scared, though. I wish there was something more I could do."

"It's not your fault she got hit," he assured her as he took a sharp curve like a pro. "We've got a lot of redtails around here, and they like to hunt at the edges of these woods. They get so focused on their meal, they don't check for cars, so most likely she ran into you instead of the other way around."

"Where did you learn so much about hawks?"

"I grew up here, so that's some of it. The behavior stuff I've learned from the folks who rehab wildlife at the rescue center. You'd be amazed what kind of critters end up there."

"Really? Like what?"

It was very unlike her to prolong any conversation beyond the absolute basics, so the curiosity she heard in her voice surprised her. Apparently, her dramatic bird encounter had unsettled her even more than she'd realized.

"Skunks, orphaned bear cubs, last week an entire possum family. Then there's the usual dogs and cats, rabbits, stuff like that. My family and I run Gallimore Stables on the other side of the property, retraining retired racehorses for new owners."

The mention of horses got her attention, and she couldn't help being intrigued by this outgoing man who'd interrupted his morning to stop and help out a complete stranger and a hawk. Feeling some of her reluctance seeping away, she took a deep breath and blurted, "My last name's Holloway."

"Pleased to meet you, Bekah Holloway." Sliding her an easygoing grin, he added, "What brings you to Oaks Crossing?"

Despite her lingering tension, she laughed. "So, that's where I am. I was trying to get to a job interview in Rockville. The receptionist gave me directions, but I got turned around somewhere and couldn't find any road signs."

"Worked out well for me." When she gave him a puzzled look, his grin widened. "If you hadn't gotten lost, I never would've met you."

She'd known more than her share of smooth talkers, and she recognized a line when she heard one. Normally, she would have let it pass since she'd never see him again. But something inside her raised up its head and pushed her to nip his subtle advance in the bud. Maybe she still had some of her dignity, after all.

Not wanting to sound rude, she came up with a polite way to set him straight. "And without you to help her, this hawk would be in major trouble. Right?"

He seemed to pick up on her meaning, and he nodded. "Right."

They made the rest of their trip in silence. While that was what she'd had in mind, Bekah was almost disappointed. Drew struck her as a genuinely decent guy willing to lend a hand where it was needed, even if it was inconvenient for him.

Unfortunately, she'd run across too many people who seemed good at first and turned out to be anything but. It had left her jaded and, by necessity, leery of—well, everyone. It was really too bad, she thought as she stared out the window at the trees flashing by. If she was someone else, she might have considered finding a job here and staying a while. A long string of personal disasters had soured her on serious relationships, but based on their quick connection, there was a chance she and Drew might have become friends.

She'd grown weary of constantly traveling from one place to another to hide her tracks, and always being an outsider was disheartening, to say the least. Now that summer was over, she'd love nothing more than to spend the winter in a nice little town way off the grid and catch her breath. The trouble was, she knew she hadn't come close to shedding her past, and she didn't have the luxury of becoming complacent. She'd have to settle for finding a reasonably safe harbor until her well-honed survival instinct warned her it was time to move on again.

It wasn't the life she wanted, but it was the one she had to live. And there was nothing she could do about that.

Bekah Holloway was a puzzle wrapped in a mystery.

To Drew, it looked as if she'd been living in her car, and the condition of it told him she was pretty hard up for money. As if that wasn't bad enough, her skittish behavior made it obvious to him that she was running from something—or someone. Slender but clearly stronger than she looked, her auburn hair and vivid blue eyes accented a pretty face with freckles sprinkled across her cheeks. In truth, she reminded him of the pixies in the stories his mother used to read him when he was a boy.

That observation drifted through Drew's mind as he snuck a glance over at her. Completely engrossed by soothing the wounded hawk, she seemed oblivious to Drew's presence. That was a new one for him, and he couldn't keep back a slight grin. Most of the time, women flirted shamelessly with him, and he obliged them by flirting back.

Being from good Irish stock, he'd always believed friendliness was in his DNA. Life was short, and he couldn't see the point in keeping anything back. Of course, that philosophy had landed him in trouble more than once, and a couple of years ago, the woman he'd loved enough to build his future around had chosen her dream career over him. With tears in her eyes, Kelly had turned down his proposal and headed for San Francisco, leaving his heart in so many pieces, he still hadn't found them all.

He wanted the strong, loving marriage his parents

had enjoyed until his father's death a few years ago, and he kept trying to find the woman to build it with. His older brother's wedding the year before had gotten him thinking about the future even more lately, but as he crept toward his thirtieth birthday, he'd started to wonder if he was destined to spend the rest of his days as everyone's favorite uncle.

He didn't really want to be stuck in his tiny hometown for the rest of forever, but his family's struggling farm needed every pair of available hands to keep it out of bankruptcy. Gallimore was more than the Kinleys' business—it was their home. Leaving to pursue his own dreams sounded good in theory, but the reality of it was he'd never be able to live with himself if his family lost the farm, and he hadn't done everything in his power to stop it.

His brooding was cut short when they reached the sign marking the Oaks Crossing Rescue Center. Turning into the lot, he parked next to a dusty two-door that was the only other car there.

Going carefully to avoid scaring either of his passengers, he got out and went around to open Bekah's door for her. She looked up at him with fearful eyes, and he smiled to reassure her. "Sierra's here, and she's the best. Your little friend will be in good hands, I promise."

A flicker of something akin to hope passed over her features. "I guess I have to trust you, don't I?"

She made it sound like a real stretch for her, which made him wonder what had happened to turn this intelligent young woman into a scared rabbit. Since he didn't have a clue how to answer her question, he walked ahead and opened the entryway door for her.

"Good morning," Sierra Walker greeted them in her characteristically chipper tone. "I'm set up for our new guest in back, so come on through."

As they walked, he introduced the two women, who traded quick nods before getting down to business. Bekah rested her bundle on an exam table, and Sierra carefully opened the soft cocoon. Seeming to anticipate a struggle, she held the bird still, talking in a singsong voice he'd heard her use with dozens of other animals.

"Hello there, beautiful," she crooned, running expert hands over the hawk. "You've had a tough morning, haven't you?"

"I'm so sorry," Bekah apologized, anguish clouding her eyes. "I never saw her until I hit her."

"I'd imagine Drew explained it was probably the other way around."

"Well, yes, but I thought he was just trying to make me feel better about hurting her."

"Actually, that's the way it usually happens, so you've got nothing to feel guilty about. They get this laser focus when they're hunting, and they don't notice anything else except their prey. Isn't that right, sweetheart?" she added to the hawk.

"So she really is a girl?" Drew asked. When she nodded, he chuckled at Bekah. "Guess you were right about that."

"And you were wrong," she retorted with more than a little venom in her tone. That set off more alarm bells in his head, warning him to steer clear of this obviously troubled young woman. He preferred sweet, uncomplicated girls whose biggest problem was choosing what outfit they were going to wear on Saturday night. Bekah, on the other hand, had already proven to have more twists than a steep mountain road. Between long days at the farm and pitching in at the center most weekends, he had plenty to deal with already, he cautioned himself. The last thing he needed was a challenge.

Still, there was something about her that reached out to him in a way he'd never experienced before. Maybe it was that she needed him, or that he'd gained enough of her trust that she'd finally gotten the nerve to share her last name with him.

Or maybe it was something else altogether. That possibility bothered him more than he cared to think about right now.

"Wouldn't be the first time," he replied smoothly, adding a grin to show there were no hard feelings on his part. She gave him an odd look, but he stubbornly kept the smile in place. He'd never let a woman get the better of him before, and he wasn't about to start now. After all, he had a well-earned reputation to protect.

"Okay, here's the deal," Sierra interrupted in a crisp way that said she meant business. "It looks like our girl has some broken bones in her left wing, so we'll wrap it to keep it stable while they heal. She also has what appears to be a decent concussion."

"Is that why her one eye isn't open very far?" Bekah asked.

"Yes, but it responds to light, so that's a good sign. Judging by her size, I'd say she's a couple of years old, strong and healthy up till now. That means that if she gets the right care, her chances of recovering and being released back into her natural environment are excellent."

"Oh, that's wonderful! I can't tell you how grateful I am to hear that." For the first time, Bekah smiled, her eyes lighting with pure joy. Pretty as she was, the fragile-looking runaway was absolutely beautiful when she smiled.

"It's what we do," Sierra told her. "Our certified wildlife rehabilitator is on her way over, and she'll know exactly what needs to be done. I set up a cage in back for the hawk, so if you bring her in, we'll get her settled and rustle up some breakfast."

"Does that sound good to you?" Bekah asked the hawk as she scooped her up from the table with more confidence than she'd shown earlier. "You probably can't wait to get out of this bag."

Once they had her safely tucked into an oversize birdcage, their patient hobbled around the papered floor, checking out her new digs. Apparently satisfied, she settled down and let out what struck him as a very human-like sigh of relief.

"She needs a name," Bekah commented in a thoughtful tone. Then, blushing as if just realizing she'd spoken out loud, she turned to Sierra with a questioning look. "Is it all right to do that?"

Normally, they only named animals who were staying at the center because they couldn't find a home or go back into the wild. Drew caught Sierra's eye and gave her a subtle nod. Bekah had clearly been having a rough time, and it seemed to him that naming the hawk might give her spirits a much-needed boost.

"Sure," Sierra replied. "What did you have in mind?"

Bekah studied the resting bird intently for a few moments, then smiled. "With all those pretty burgundy-and-white feathers, I think she looks like a Rosie."

"Rosie it is." Grabbing an index card and permanent marker, Sierra wrote down the name, date and her estimate of the age. When she was finished, she asked, "Would you like to help me get her breakfast together?"

"That depends," Bekah hedged. "What are you planning to feed her?"

"Raw chicken and water for now. When she's feeling stronger, we'll move on to live meals, but that'll be a while."

"Chicken and water I can handle."

With that decided, she held Drew's sweatshirt out for him. When he saw the condition it was in, he chuckled and held up his hands. "That's okay. She can keep it."

"It's my fault it got ruined, so I'll buy you a new one." It was a sweet offer, but he could tell by the hesitance in her eyes that she really couldn't afford it.

"Not necessary. I'm happy to give my shirt to a lady anytime." As soon as those words left his mouth, he realized they could be easily misunderstood to mean he went around handing his shirts to random women. Feeling foolish, he quickly added, "I mean, if she needs it for some reason."

What was wrong with him? It wasn't like him to lose his cool and just blurt things out that way. A strong dose of caffeine was probably in order, he reasoned. Not to mention a shower.

"Okay." Bekah gave him a long, suspicious look, then a tentative smile. "Thank you."

"No problem." He caught Sierra studying him with a curious expression, and he brushed it off with a grin. "Need anything else while I'm here?"

"I've got twelve kennels to clean before we open, and I still haven't fed all of the wild babies yet."

It was a common problem for them here. As a non-profit clinic, they relied on donations and grants to keep everything going. That meant they couldn't pay the staff much, and consistent volunteers were hard to come by. They'd recently lost their veterinarian, and animals of every species kept pouring in from the surrounding area every week. Shorthanded didn't come close to describing the situation, and Drew made it a point to lend a hand whenever he could spare the time. "I've got an hour before anyone will miss me in the barns."

"That would be awesome. Thanks."

To his complete surprise, the timid woman he'd met less than an hour ago piped up with, "Are you looking for help around here?"

Sierra flashed him a questioning glance, and he shrugged to say it was her call. Bekah had astonished him, too, but he couldn't help noticing how she was now looking Sierra directly in the eye. Standing up straighter, too, instead of trying to make herself as small and invisible as possible.

After a few seconds, the clinic's manager replied, "We're always looking for help. Mind if I ask what kind of job experience you have?"

"I'm not trained for anything in particular, but I'm a hard worker, and I learn fast. I was working at Jennings's farm stand until last week when they closed for the fall. Mr. Jennings said I could use him as a reference."

"He's an old friend of the family." Drew added

his two cents without hesitation. "He's pretty hard to please, so if he likes your work, you're a keeper."

That got him another, slightly warmer smile from Bekah, and then she turned to Sierra. "I'll work a week for nothing, so you can check my references and make sure I'm right for the job."

The desperation in her voice was impossible to miss, and it took all of Drew's self-control not to pull rank and tell her she was hired. Technically, the Kinleys owned the center, and Sierra worked for them. Realistically, she was in charge of the clinic and its operation, and they'd never stepped in to tell her what to do. He wasn't keen on changing that arrangement, but something about Bekah made him want to go a few extra steps for her.

While the two women talked about what the position involved, one of his late father's favorite lines drifted through his memory.

Do unto others as you would have them do unto you.

Drew recalled hearing that more than once growing up, when his quick temper got the better of him, and he ended up fighting with one of his brothers or a kid at school who was pestering him. Mike was the oldest, and Josh was the youngest, so they had it easy. Erin was the only girl, which made her the princess. As the middle son, Drew had learned early on that he had a simple choice: he could either live up to his big brother's solid example or overcome it and be his own person.

He was still wrestling with that one, and he often wished Dad was still around to give him advice. Whether he'd follow it or not was up for debate, but he would've appreciated the input. Unfortunately, now it was too late.

Shrugging off his suddenly melancholy mood, he refocused on the conversation that had continued along quite nicely without him. Bekah's delicate appearance had thrown him at first, but the spirit he saw glowing in her eyes had drawn him much closer than he normally would've gone after such an odd first meeting. The fading bruise on her cheek infuriated him, and he honestly hoped he never discovered who was responsible for it. It wouldn't go well for the monster who'd struck her hard enough to leave such an ugly mark behind.

To his great relief, Sierra finally appeared satisfied and shook Bekah's hand to seal their arrangement. "Let's go find a pair of coveralls that fit you. You're going to need them."

Chapter Two

Bekah wasn't at all sure what to make of Drew Kinley.

Still dressed in the tank top and beat-up cargo shorts he was wearing when they met earlier that morning, he started working with her around seven o'clock and kept on going. He didn't try to draw her into conversation but kept his comments to whatever task they were doing at the moment. He was pleasant and upbeat but didn't go out of his way to make her talk to him.

Most people took her long silences as either rude or evidence that something was bothering her. It was nice to meet someone who understood her reserved nature and accepted it for what it was.

At one point, he fetched them each some bottled water. After a long swallow, he stopped long enough to call someone named Mike. "What can I say, big brother? They need a hand down here, and I'm sure you won't miss fighting with me all that much." After a pause, he chuckled. "Yeah, it'll earn me some brownie points with Erin, too. Don't think that didn't occur to me. See ya later."

He pocketed his phone and turned back to the straw he was pitching into several stalls set aside for larger animals. In the section he'd referred to as the nursery, three goats and a wide-eyed fawn watched him from their temporary quarters in a storage area with a Dutch door. They looked to be assessing his work, and despite the odd turn her day had taken, Bekah felt herself smiling at the image.

She hadn't done much of that lately, she realized. There hadn't been all that much to lift her spirits the past few months, and when she thought about it, meeting Drew was the highlight of her year. Pathetic, but true. He'd been so nice to her, she decided she should make more of an effort to be sociable. What better topic to start with than the woman he'd just mentioned wanting to impress?

"So," Bekah commented in what she hoped came across as friendly interest. "Is Erin your girlfriend?"

He gave her the blankest look she'd ever seen in her life, then broke out laughing. "Not even close. She's my little sister and the bane of my existence. If I can do something to get on her good side for a change, I will. So a little extra work is totally worth a few days of peace from her."

Watching him banter back and forth with Sierra had made it plain they were nothing more than friends. For some reason, Bekah was ridiculously pleased to discover this incredibly charming man was unattached. Not that it should make any difference to her, she told herself sternly. She wouldn't be in town long enough for it to matter whether he was single or not. She was just making conversation. "So, this place was your sister's idea?"

"Yeah. It's her pet project."

He angled his head to glance over at her, and she saw humor twinkling in his eyes. When she got the joke, she groaned. "That's a terrible pun."

"Doesn't mean it's not true," he assured her with a shameless grin. Spreading more straw, he asked, "So, what kind of job were you interviewing for over in Rockville?"

"The kind that pays." Hearing the angry bite in her tone, Bekah winced. "Sorry, that was rude. There was some light factory work I thought I could manage. I'm sure they've filled the spot by now."

"Where are you staying?"

In my car, she nearly blurted before realizing that was more than he needed to know. Beyond that, it made her sound pathetic, and she didn't want him feeling sorry for her. As her feisty Grams used to say, she was down but not out. At least not yet. "I'm looking for a place that doesn't break the bank. Do you have any recommendations?"

"I might. Depends on you, I guess."

What a curious thing to say. In spite of herself, she had to admit he'd snagged her interest with that one. She stopped cleaning the water bottles that hung in the cages for smaller animals and looked over at him. "What do you mean?"

Resting his arms across the handle of his pitchfork, he explained. "You seem to like the animals here."

"Definitely," she answered with a nod. "To be deadly honest, I like animals better than people."

"Yeah? Why's that?"

"They don't judge you or make you feel stupid when you mess things up." One of the scruffy pygmy goats went up on his hind legs and rested his tiny front hoofs on the dividing wall. Reaching over, she scratched between his sprouting horns with a smile. "All they want is to be fed and have a safe place to sleep. Whoever gives them that is their hero, and they love you to pieces."

Drew didn't respond to that, and she glanced over to find him studying her with a somber expression. An angry glint appeared in his eyes again, and she recognized it from when he'd noticed the healing bruise on her cheek. It vanished as quickly as it had appeared, but his grim look stayed in place.

"Are you talking about these critters," he asked gently, "or yourself?"

His perceptiveness was unnerving, to say the least, and she clamped her mouth shut to avoid stammering in shock. Once she regained some of her composure, she replied, "Let's just say I can relate to where they're coming from. I've been in some places that I have no intention of ever going back to."

"Making a better life for yourself," he added, eyes now twinkling with approval. "Good for you."

"I hope so. Seeing as I don't have much choice but to keep going forward."

She wasn't usually so honest with someone she barely knew, and she held her breath waiting for him to ask her to clarify what on earth she was talking about. Instead, he gave her an encouraging smile that warmed her all over.

"That's a great way to look at it," he said. "I think that's a good strategy for all of us."

Did he really? she wondered, or was he just being nice? As he got back to work in the stalls, she pondered their brief discussion in an attempt to sort through her conflicting feelings about him. She'd grown so accustomed to guys who said what they thought she wanted to hear, she was constantly on her guard around them. Because of that, she wasn't sure how to read Drew's wide-open, friendly personality.

Could it be that by some crazy stroke of fortune, she'd stumbled across a truly honest, straightforward man who said what he meant and meant what he said? Stranger things had happened, she supposed. She just couldn't recall the last time they'd happened to her.

While she was lost in her brooding, the end door swung open, and Sierra came through lugging two old-fashioned milk bottle carriers filled with what looked like large plastic baby bottles topped with oversize nipples. The residents of the baby section went bananas, bleating and calling for their breakfast while Drew hurried forward to lend a hand.

"Those look kinda heavy," he said as he took them from her.

"They are," she acknowledged, a bit breathless. "Thanks for the help."

"Well, you know how that works."

Narrowing her eyes, she nailed him with a suspicious glare. "I'm not doing your laundry like I had to when my poor Angels lost the World Series to Cincinnati."

"Nah, nothin' like that," he assured her smoothly, setting the formula down on a nearby hay bale.

"Then what?"

"We'll talk about it later," he said with a wink. "Who gets fed first?"

"I think he does," Bekah replied, laughing as the

determined pygmy goat climbed on his buddy's back trying to get at the bottles.

"You can start with him," Sierra agreed.

When her meaning sank in, Bekah shook her head. "You mean, you want me to do it?"

"Sure. They know how to eat, so you just hold the bottle up for them and wait till they're done." Bleating up a storm, the little goat was butting his head against the wall, and she laughed. "Here, let me show you."

She climbed into the pen and lifted him out. Grabbing a bottle, she set him on his feet and sat down on the sawdust-covered dirt floor beside him. Eager for his breakfast, he latched on to the nipple and sucked down the formula like it was his last meal.

"Wow, he's really going to town," Bekah commented, patting his wiry brindle coat while he ate. "Are they all this easy?"

"The trick is to keep them from running over each other or you. They're not starving or anything, but babies don't like to wait in line, do they?" Sierra cooed, tapping him on his forehead while he gazed up at her with adoring eyes. Right then and there, Bekah decided she wanted to experience that kind of heroine worship for herself.

Hoping to make a good impression on her prospective new boss, without being told, she clambered into the pen the way Sierra had and cradled another goat in her arms. Drew held out his hands, and while she appreciated his gesture, she firmly shook her head. "I've got it."

"They squirm a lot, y'know," he cautioned her.

"That's okay. I'm stronger than I look."

Approval flashed across Sierra's face, and she met

Bekah's eyes with a quick nod. Feeling as though she'd made some progress, Bekah carefully brought out the hornless goat and set her down, settling beside her the way Sierra had done. Really, all she had to do was hold up the bottle, and the little goat did the rest.

Apparently satisfied, Sierra stood and brushed off her jeans with her hands. "Well, it looks like you're good to go. I'll have a chat with Drew and come back in a few. Just remember—one at a time. Otherwise, they'll stampede all over the place, and we'll have a horrible time catching them."

Bekah noticed the woman had implied that if she made a mistake, Sierra would help her corral the escapees. Used to fending for herself, she found it comforting to know someone would have her back if she needed them.

Rubbing the back of the slurping goat, she replied, "Oh, we'll be fine, won't we, little one?"

"Keep telling yourself that, and it'll be true," Drew told her with a smile. "I've gotta get going. Thanks to Rosie, I'm later for work than usual."

"I don't know the first thing about horses," she confided. "It must be a fun job."

"Some days yes, some days no. Today we've gotta move a dozen or so of our boarders so we can do some maintenance in their barn."

"That sounds dangerous."

"Nah. We've got a real steady Belgian draft horse named Gideon who's seen it all, so he never gets rattled by anything, no matter how bad the others think it is. My brother Mike just marches him out first, and the rest of them trail after him like puppies."

She couldn't help laughing at the picture he painted. "Those are some seriously large puppies."

"Most of 'em aren't a problem when you know how to handle 'em. Mike's some kind of horse whisperer, so the rest of us just follow his lead."

Although his delivery was upbeat, she picked up on something below the surface that didn't sound right to her. Inspiration struck, and she asked, "Do you ever get to be in charge when it comes to the horses?"

He looked surprised, then shook his head with a grin. "Man, you've got me pegged. The horses are his territory, and I'm more like a foot soldier."

"What about the rescue center? You seem to know where everything is, so I'm guessing you put in a lot of time over here."

"I like animals in general," he said, scratching the head of a nosy miniature alpaca, "so I enjoy working here when I have the time. But Sierra's in charge."

"If you could be your own boss, what kind of business would you have?"

"Something outside," he replied immediately, as if he'd thought about it often enough that the answer came easily to him. "Maybe a wilderness guide out west or something. I visited Mike in New Mexico once, and I couldn't believe how incredible the desert and the mountains are. Totally different from what I'm used to, but really beautiful."

His tone had shifted ever so slightly, the gold in his eyes warming as he stared down at her. At first, Bekah couldn't define what had changed, then she replayed his words in her mind and wondered if he was referring to something other than the Western scenery.

"Anyway," he went on as if nothing unusual had

happened, "Sierra usually comes down to the house for lunch around noon. You're welcome to join us if you want, meet the rest of our nutty crew."

Out of necessity, she'd learned not to depend on anyone for anything. But he'd been so kind to her, she decided it was okay to bend that rule just this one time. "Thanks. That sounds good."

"I'll see you then."

Giving her another encouraging smile, he followed Sierra from the shed, leaving Bekah in charge of feeding the babies. Glancing around, she counted heads and came up with twelve. Two down, ten to go. Surrounded by endless noise and questionable smells, she knew that some people might consider this the worst job in the world.

But to Bekah, this little barn tucked into the backwoods of Kentucky was like paradise, protected from the outside world and bursting with promising new lives. She couldn't imagine any place she'd rather be.

"Now," Drew began when he and Sierra were alone out front. "I don't want to tell you how to run this place…"

"But you want me to hire Bekah," she finished for him. The doubt in her dark eyes made it clear what she thought of his idea, but she didn't say anything else.

Two could play that game, Drew mused. Fortunately—or unfortunately, depending on how you looked at it, sparring with his last girlfriend had left him a master at verbal fencing. "Yeah."

"Why?"

Oh, she was good. Warming to the challenge she was laying in front of him, he said, "I'm not sure. I've just got a feeling about her."

"Again? How many is that this year?"

His reputation as a lady killer had been well-earned, and he laughed. "Not that kind of feeling. I mean she seems like she's had a rough time of it lately, and she needs a safe place to land."

While his mind accepted that explanation without question, his Irish heart had another idea altogether. This morning, he'd taken a route for his run that he hadn't used in months and had hit that section of road just after Bekah's frightening encounter with Rosie. Something—or someone—had brought them together for a reason. He might not understand why just yet, but he couldn't shake the belief that he and the enigmatic runaway were meant to connect on that lonely back road.

He and Sierra stared at each other for several seconds, until she finally broke the silence. "I don't know."

"Aw, come on," he pleaded, which was a big stretch for him. He made it a point never to want anything so badly he'd get down on his knees for it. But this was different. Every instinct he had was warning him that Bekah was in trouble and needed help. His help. "She stopped to take care of a hawk that dive-bombed her car and scared her half to death. You've seen for yourself how great she is with the animals."

"We've stretched our budget as far as it will go this year. I can't pay her much more than nothing until January."

"I don't think that's an issue for her. She just needs a job."

"We don't know anything about her. She could be in trouble, or running from the police or something."

The image of that fading bruise refused to leave

him alone, and he frowned. "She's definitely running from something, but my gut tells me it's not the law."

"Are you kidding me? I'm supposed to hire someone for a sensitive job like this based on your gut?"

She had a point, he had to admit, and knowing his family, they'd agree with her. Then a solution hit him. "I've got a buddy who works in the county sheriff's office. I can have him run a background check on her, off the record. Would that make you feel better?"

"I guess."

He could tell he had her on the ropes. Sierra was a caring soul with a generous heart, and he knew she felt genuine sympathy for their mysterious visitor. Now to knock her over the edge and get a full-on yes for his true plan. "One more thing."

"Here it comes," she grumbled, glaring up at him. It was a good thing they were such solid friends, or he'd have been worried she might smack him. "What?"

"Judging by the condition her car's in, I'm pretty sure she needs a place to stay."

"Don't look at me like that, Lancelot," Sierra retorted crisply. "My studio apartment's more like a closet with a futon in it."

"Okay, then I'll ask Mom. I'm sure she can find a spot for Bekah at the house till we come up with something better."

"Like what?"

Drew mulled the problem over for a minute, then grinned. "What about the old stable manager's office out back? It's got a bunk and its own bathroom, along with a small kitchen. I can get a mattress from Mom, and her old fridge is still on the service porch, just waiting to be donated."

"That room's filthy, and no one's used it in years."

"So it's perfect. Bekah won't be in anyone's way, and she can have some privacy. Beyond that," he added, going in for the kill, "she'll be on-site all the time. Once she's trained, she can take over the morning chores, and you won't have to come in at the crack of dawn. Ever."

Glowering at his logic, Sierra opened her mouth to protest, then slowly closed it. She chewed on his proposal for a minute and finally relented with a sigh. "Okay, we'll give her a try. *After* your friend checks her out," she added, stabbing Drew's chest with a finger for emphasis. "I'm responsible for this center and every one of the animals living here. I won't risk all that because you've got a feeling about a girl."

"Like I told you," he retorted, "it's not *that* kind of feeling."

She gave him a long, dubious look that clearly said she didn't believe him. As she went back into the rear shed to finish doling out breakfast, he put her irritating reaction out of his mind. Right now he had more important things to worry about.

Pulling out his phone, he thumbed down to the number he needed and pressed Dial. A crisp, professional voice answered, and he grinned. "Harley? Is that you? You sound like some rich guy's uptight butler." That got him a less than charitable reply, and he chuckled. "Hey, I need a favor, unofficially. I don't know—cover your monitor or something. Here's what I need."

Once he explained, Harley put him on hold to do a quick search of some mystical police database that would at least reveal whether or not Bekah was on the most-wanted list. Subjected to an instrumental version of a creaky old ballad, Drew strolled around the lobby until Harley came back on the line. "Your girl's clear as far as I can see. Not even a parking ticket."

"Awesome. Thanks, man. I owe you one."

"I'll add it to the list," his childhood friend assured him with a chuckle. "Take 'er easy."

"You, too."

Clicking his phone off as he walked through an unmarked door, he found Sierra measuring out antibiotics for some patient or another. She held up her index finger for him to wait, and when she was finished, she looked up at him. "I can tell by the delighted look on your face that you got the answer you wanted to hear."

"From what Harley could tell, Bekah's record is clean as a whistle. I'm way overdue at the farm, but I'm gonna head out back and see how that old plumbing looks. I wouldn't want to overstay my welcome and step on your pretty little toes."

"Oh, you're a real prince. You owe me one, Kinley boy."

Echoing what he'd told Harley, he shot back, "Just add it to the list."

"Don't worry. I will."

Bekah didn't have a watch, but the sun was directly overhead when she and Sierra finally finished taking care of all the animals and their pens. Everything was clean, everyone had been fed and dosed, and at one o'clock they had a family coming in to take home the adorable black lab puppy they'd chosen to adopt. Not long after that, Sierra had told her, it would be time to do it all over again and get everyone tucked in for the night.

Never a dull moment at the rescue center, Bekah thought with a grin. She loved it.

"Okay, rookie," Sierra announced briskly. "Lunchtime."

"I'm fine."

"There are laws in this state, and one of them says I can't work you to death. Unless I feed you first," she added with a wink. "Fortunately for you, it won't be my cooking you have to stomach. Maggie Kinley's the best cook in the county, and she's always got room for one more. If you don't mind walking over to the house, we can chat on the way."

That sounded promising, so Bekah agreed and quickly washed her hands at a nearby utility sink. Outside, a mild autumn breeze rustled through the trees behind the center, shaking more leaves loose to float lazily down to the ground.

Leaving the cluster of barns where she'd spent her morning, she followed Sierra onto a dirt lane that wound through acres of white-fenced bluegrass with horses of every size and color peacefully grazing in the sunlight. At the other end she saw a rambling white farmhouse surrounded by well-tended gardens. With wide porches and baskets of flowers hanging along the roofline, it had a welcoming look that invited people to stop in and visit for a while.

"You've done great today," Sierra began in her brisk, efficient way. "I threw every job I could at you, and you handled them better than anyone I've ever seen. You've got a real way with animals."

Unaccustomed to being praised for simply doing as she'd been told, Bekah felt prouder than she had in a long time. She didn't want to come across as being needy, though, so she kept her response simple. "Thank you."

Sierra gave her a sidelong glance and shook her head with a smile. "You're welcome. I know you've only been with us part of a day, but were you serious about wanting something more permanent?"

Excited beyond words, Bekah clamped her mouth shut before she could make a complete fool of herself and destroy Sierra's positive view of her. Taking a deep breath to steady her voice, she said, "What did you have in mind?"

"It'd be great to find someone who could be at the clinic when I'm not. Sometimes things come up after I've left for the day, and I don't know anything's happened until morning."

Bekah heard what she wasn't saying and frowned. "You mean an animal might take a turn for the worst, and by the time you find out, it's too late to help them?"

"Yeah," Sierra acknowledged sadly. "I live in Rockville and take night classes, so it's not possible for me to be at the center 24/7."

The regret in her voice made Bekah want to do something to ease her mind. Beyond that, working at the clinic would let her keep an eye on Rosie while she healed. Despite Drew and Sierra's assurances, she felt a deep sense of responsibility for the wounded hawk.

Still, she hated to make a commitment she couldn't keep, so she chose her words very carefully. "I'm not sure how long I'll be in town, but I can cover the open hours at the clinic until you find someone else for the job."

"Fabulous." Sierra named an hourly rate a few cents above minimum wage, punctuating that with an apologetic shrug. "I know it's not much, but that's honestly the best I can do. The good news is rooms in town aren't expensive, so you should be able to find a place to stay."

Once her car was fixed, anyway, Bekah thought grimly. Shaking off the pessimism that had become an ugly habit for her, she decided to start focusing on the good instead of the bad. "I'll take it. And thank you for giving me a chance. I'm sure I'm not your first choice."

"Honey, you're my only choice," her new boss confided, wrapping an arm around her shoulders in a quick hug. "If we both put our minds to it, we'll figure out a way to make it work."

"I'm good at that."

That comment got her a long, appraising look from the upbeat woman who'd just unwittingly saved Bekah from an uncertain future. "That doesn't surprise me in the least."

They chatted pleasantly the rest of the way and stopped at the foot of the back porch steps. The door was open, and through the wood-framed screen Bekah heard what sounded like an army talking, laughing and generally making a ruckus. Over it all, she barely heard a woman's voice shout, "Lunch is ready!"

Sierra climbed up to the porch, but Bekah's feet refused to move even an inch. "Sierra?" When she turned back, Bekah asked, "How many people are in there?"

"Oh, usually ten or fifteen, depending. There's no school today, so there might be some kids, too. Why?"

Bekah didn't want to seem ungrateful, but the thought of facing so many strangers just about paralyzed her. While she was trying to come up with a polite way to decline, she heard footsteps approaching from behind her.

"Hello, ladies," Drew's mellow voice drawled. "Glad you could make it."

Turning to face him, she felt an unfamiliar hitch in her stomach. His hair was damp, and he'd changed from his running clothes into jeans and a pale green T-shirt that made his eyes glitter like emeralds. A full head taller than her, he had the solid look of someone who'd worked outside his entire life. As he approached her, she was vaguely aware of Sierra continuing up the steps, effectively leaving her alone with the best-looking man she'd ever met.

Why hadn't she noticed that before? she asked herself. Oh, right, between Rosie and her whirlwind morning at the clinic, she'd been too busy to do much more than glance at him. Now that she had a chance for a better look, it was pathetically obvious she'd missed a few details that morning. Quite a few.

When she realized he was waiting for her to say something, she felt her cheeks warming with embarrassment. She hadn't paid much attention to the niceties lately, and apparently her social skills had withered a bit. Hoping to cover her slip with a bright smile, she said, "Thanks for the invitation. I didn't have breakfast this morning, so I'm famished."

"Then we better get you inside before you drop," he teased, going ahead to open the door for her. When she didn't follow, he nudged her. "After you."

Coming from him, the old-fashioned gesture caught her by surprise. Mr. Jennings had behaved that way toward her, but he was old enough to be her grandfather, and she'd assumed that was the explanation for his gallant treatment of her. Apparently, it was a Southern thing, she mused with a slight grin. Definitely something a girl could get used to.

So with Drew standing solidly behind her, she waded into the most chaotic scene she'd ever experienced outside of an after-Christmas sale. A quick glance around showed her that Sierra hadn't been exaggerating about the number of people. She saw everyone from dusty farmhands to an adorable blond girl sitting at the table with a slender woman, coloring pictures in a book as if there wasn't a storm of activity swirling around them.

An older woman was mixing a salad on the huge prep island, and she looked up when the screen door slapped closed. Instantly, she put on a huge smile and wiped her hands on a towel as she came around to greet them.

"You must be Bekah," she said warmly, shaking her hand and beaming as if she'd just come across a long-lost daughter. "Drew called to tell me you might be coming in for lunch. I'm Maggie Kinley, and on a good day I'm in charge around here. Today I'm not so sure."

Dredging up her rusty manners, Bekah did her best to smile back. "It's nice to meet you."

"Mom's the ringleader of this little circus," Drew explained with a chuckle. Pointing to a tall man at the head of the table, he said, "That's my big brother Mike, baby brother Josh…"

"Who wishes you'd quit calling him that," a slightly slimmer version of the older two protested. "I'm twenty-five, y'know."

"Whatever."

Josh growled, and Drew grinned back, clearly not concerned in the least. He went on to introduce the little girl as his niece, Abby, and the lovely woman beside her as Mike's wife, Lily.

After that, the names and faces blurred together in a mishmash of strangers Bekah was fairly certain she'd never be able to keep straight. But she doggedly smiled and nodded at each one, trying to look more confident than she felt. "It's nice to meet you all."

"You look dead on your feet, honey," Maggie clucked, patting the end of one of the long benches flanking the table. "Can I get you something to drink?"

"I got it, Mom," Drew answered, opening the fridge to take out a humongous pitcher. "What would you say to some lemonade, Bekah?"

In reply, she held out an empty glass, and he laughed. "Yes, ma'am."

While he filled it and added ice, it struck her that she'd actually done something he thought was funny. After spending months skulking from one town to the next, doing everything in her power to keep from drawing attention to herself, she was pleased to discover she hadn't completely lost her sense of humor.

This bright, comfortable feeling might not last, she acknowledged, but for now it felt good. And that was enough for her.

In a stroke of rare genius, Drew took the end seat, leaving Bekah next to his bubbly sister-in-law. They talked easily enough, and his worry about her ebbed a bit. As a kindergarten teacher, Lily was used to dealing with all kinds of personalities in her students, and she was as accepting a person as he'd ever met. She'd have to be, he mused with a wry grin. Mike was a good guy, but he wasn't exactly Mr. Congeniality.

"So, Drew, are we gonna see you here on the farm sometime today?" the ogre in question asked from the other end of the table.

Drew recognized that he'd been pushing it all morning, even though he believed he'd been doing something more important than whatever Mike had planned for him. But he didn't want to start one of their notorious arguments in front of their skittish guest, so he brushed away his annoyance. "I got a few more things to finish at the clinic, but they can wait till tomorrow. So I'm all yours."

"We're almost done with the hay," Josh informed him around a mouthful of salad. "Then we'll be out fixing the line of fencing those crazy ponies took down during yesterday's thunderstorm."

"We should replace that wire with board fences," Drew commented to no one in particular.

"If we could afford it, we would," Mike reminded him with a scowl. "Since we can't, we can't."

Bold, blatant logic, and an everyday fact of life at Gallimore Stables. Someday, Drew hoped they could manage the farm the right way, instead of barely holding things together with their bare hands.

When Dad had been alive and training racehorses, they'd never worried about money or how they were going to keep the place going. Now, it seemed like they never quit worrying about it. As much as he loved the farm, sometimes he got tired of the constant pressure they were all under to keep the numbers from sliding too far into the red.

Those were the times he couldn't help wondering if there might be a better life for him somewhere else. Then his innate loyalty kicked in, and he plastered on a smile while he kept trudging along, waiting for things to improve enough for him to strike out on his own.

"Then I'll meet you and Josh out in the back pasture," he said matter-of-factly. Stringing a mile of fence was the last thing he wanted to do, but he was confident that his brothers weren't thrilled about it, either. Since there was no point grumbling about what had to be done, he switched topics. "On the radio this morning, I heard Tennessee's favored against Dallas this Sunday. I'm not sure about that one."

"Dallas is using a backup quarterback who's never started a pro game, so they might be right."

The comment came from—of all people—Bekah. She sounded like she knew what she was talking about, and he eyed her with new respect. "You speak football?"

"I'm from Chicago," she informed him with a smirk. "Speaking football is a requirement."

"Is that right?" Fascinated, he folded his arms on the table and grinned at her. "Any thoughts on the San Fran game Monday night?"

"They'll lose. They're playing in Seattle, which has the loudest home fans in the country. Opponents can never hear a thing in that stadium, and the San Fran front line is full of rookies who won't be able to communicate well enough to coordinate their moves. They don't stand a chance."

They kept chatting back and forth while they ate,

and he was amazed by how much she knew about his favorite sport. At one point, he teased, "It's too bad you weren't a boy. You would've made a great quarterback."

"Which Drew would know," Maggie added, ruffling his hair in a proud mom gesture. "He was an All-State quarterback all four years in high school."

"Really?" Bekah commented, lifting a curious eyebrow. "That's impressive."

Normally, he'd take that kind of praise and run with it, but today something stopped him. He didn't want her to think he was conceited, so he deflected her comment with a grin. "I had a great offensive line, and my senior year we got some sure-handed receivers. Like Josh," he added, nodding at his younger brother.

"Won the state championship that season," Josh chimed in right on cue. "Drew was MVP."

"Wow," was all Bekah said, but he picked up on something in her eyes he hadn't seen before. It reminded him of the way Lily had looked at Mike when they were first getting to know each other, a combination of interest and amusement. Even though he knew that kind of realization should make him nervous, Drew was surprised to find it didn't.

In fact, it was doing the exact opposite. He knew next to nothing about Bekah Holloway or why she was affecting him this way. Then and there, he promised himself that somehow he'd solve that little mystery so it wouldn't keep on bugging him.

And then, he'd put it past him, and his life would go back to the way it was before he met her. As someone who'd made a habit of effortlessly moving from one girl to the next, that very pragmatic strategy for handling her should have comforted him.

But it didn't. And for the life of him, he didn't know why.

His rambling thoughts were put on hold when his mother caught his eye and gave him a questioning look. He came back with a slight nod, and very casually she said, "Bekah, I think we need to figure out where you're going to sleep tonight."

"It's warm enough," she replied in a bright tone that sounded forced to him. "My car will work until I get my first paycheck."

Lily frowned in disapproval, and she added a shake of her head for effect. "Not for me, it won't. Abby?" The way his niece perked up, Drew guessed her stepmother had primed her for what was coming next. "How would you like to bunk with your dad and me for a few nights?"

"You mean, like camping? That sounds like fun."

Oh, she was good, Drew thought, barely smothering a grin. He'd have to take her for ice cream later as a reward for being such a great sport.

"I can't let you do that," Bekah protested, obviously uncomfortable with the idea. "Abby needs her sleep for school tomorrow."

"And you need yours for work," Lily reminded her in the gentle but firm tone Drew had heard her use with the students in Gallimore's riding school. "It's only temporary, until you can find a place of your own."

From the concern in Bekah's eyes, Drew knew his suspicions about her dire financial straits had been spot-on. Even with the job at the clinic, she might not be able to afford rent, much less the repairs her car needed to be driveable. Tonight when he was done at the farm, he'd go back to the rescue center and pick up where he left off.

Bekah had endured enough temporary situations to last her a while. It was high time someone stepped up and gave her something she could count on.

Chapter Three

The rest of her first day at the rescue center raced by in a flash. Bekah was so exhausted, she took a shower, fell into Abby's twin bed, and slept like a corpse until morning. When she woke, the sun was fully up, and the house was so quiet, she could hear birds twittering in the trees outside.

Abby's room was a charming combination of princess and tomboy, with pale yellow walls and pretty lace curtains fluttering beside the open windows. She had shelves full of dolls, stuffed animals and model horses whose riders were posed in a variety of daredevil moves. One set was a beautiful chestnut arching over a tall jump while the rider's blond ponytail streamed out behind her.

Since her young hostess was also blonde, Bekah assumed Abby pictured herself doing the same thing someday. Having dreams was wonderful, she mused wistfully. As long as they had a chance of coming true. This was the kind of room she'd longed to have when she was a little girl, Bekah recalled with more than a little envy. Unfortunately, her few childhood possessions had rarely made it out of their boxes before she and her vagabond family had been forced to move from their current sketchy situation to another one elsewhere.

Growing up here would've been like paradise for her. One day, she vowed, she'd figure out a way to create a home like this, with a good man who would love her no matter what. Their children would always be able to collect things that were important to them, knowing they wouldn't have to be left behind later.

But for now, she had a job to get to. She got up and made the bed, careful to put everything back exactly where she'd found it last night. After a quick shower, she pulled on a set of clean clothes and followed the scent of fresh coffee and baked goods into the kitchen. There, she found a basket of still-warm muffins on the kitchen table with a note.

Bekah—In town grocery shopping. Help yourself to whatever you want. Maggie

For a few seconds, she stared at the obviously homemade breakfast, then at the very trusting note Drew's mother had left for her. Having grown accustomed to fending for herself in every way, she couldn't believe that the woman had not only left her alone in the house, but cared enough about a total stranger to leave her something to eat. In her world, people simply didn't do this sort of thing, and she had a tough time wrapping her head around the concept.

Finally, she accepted that Maggie Kinley had indeed done both of those remarkable things, and turned the note over. She honestly wasn't sure what to write, so she went with an old standard. *Thanks so much—Bekah.*

At first, she grabbed just one muffin and poured some coffee into one of the to-go cups standing next to the stainless steel double-pot coffeemaker. Then she remembered what Sierra had said about having class last night and hunted up a container that would hold four of the delicious-smelling muffins. If it weren't for the generous vet tech in training, Bekah knew she'd still be wandering the area searching for an unskilled job where the boss wouldn't question her background too closely. It seemed that the least she could do was bring the hardworking young woman something to eat.

When she arrived at the clinic, she found Sierra in the lobby, handing an empty birdcage back to a woman with three young children in tow. "You did a good thing, bringing that squirrel here. We'll take good care of the little guy, and when his leg is healed up, we can set him free in the woods."

"Can you call us when you do that?" the oldest girl asked. She looked to be about Abby's age, and her eyes were fixed on the critter she'd clearly become attached to. "I want to say goodbye."

Sierra glanced at the mom for her permission, and the woman nodded. "I explained why we couldn't keep him, but I think it would be nice for them to see for themselves that he's back where he belongs."

"Will do. I've got your contact info, so I'll call when we're ready to release him."

"Thank you. Have a good day."

Adding a quick smile for Bekah, the woman shepherded her kids out to a minivan that looked like it had a lot of miles on it. The girl gazed longingly back into the lobby, then reluctantly climbed into her seat and disappeared when her mother slid the door shut.

"Wow, that was tough," Bekah commented in sympathy. "Is it always that hard?"

"No, but the kids really get to me. They see a fuzzy friend they can play with, but he's a wild animal, not a Disney character." Pausing, she took a deep breath and sighed. "Are those Maggie's fabulous jumbo muffins?"

"And coffee," Bekah added, setting the basket on the counter. Glancing at the clock on the wall, she saw it was nearly eight. "I'm not sure if I'm late or not, so I thought I'd bring them just in case. How was your class last night?"

"Impossibly mind-boggling." Blowing on her coffee to cool it, the clinic's director took a long, grateful sip. "I'm great with all the practical stuff because I do it here every day. The biology and anatomy terms just don't stick in my head. I desperately need a tutor, but I can't find one whose schedule meshes with mine."

Munching on a cranberry muffin so moist she barely had to chew it, Bekah pondered a possible solution to Sierra's problem. Recalling what Drew had said about his sister-in-law, she said, "What about Lily? She's a teacher. Maybe she can help get you through the rough parts."

"That's brilliant! I don't know why I didn't think of that."

Bekah had never been called brilliant in her life, and it was rewarding to know she'd helped someone who'd been so kind to her. Thoughts of kindness led her to a problem she'd been pondering since she woke up. "Sierra, I have a big favor to ask."

"Shoot."

"I've only got one day's worth of clean clothes left, and I hate to ask Mrs. Kinley for anything more. Could I do a couple loads of laundry in the machines here?"

"Sure, but ick." She made a disgusted face. "We wash all the animals' blankets and towels in those. I wouldn't put my clothes in them, that's for sure. I remember hearing they were doing some renovations at the Oaks Café on Main Street and were planning to put in a connected Laundromat. I don't know if it's finished yet, but you could check."

The mere idea of going into Oaks Crossing on her own made Bekah slightly nauseous. People would ask her all manner of questions she'd prefer not to answer, which meant she'd either have to deflect them or outright lie about her less-than-glorious background. She feared the trip would end up being a complete disaster.

That left her imposing on the Kinleys. Again. Not the ideal solution, but once she'd gotten all her clothes clean, she'd have some time to come up with a better one. While they ate, they chatted about the various animals housed at the center, and Sierra gave Bekah a brief lesson on the computer system they used to track everything from food and supply orders to wildlife release dates.

She was no computer expert, but she'd used enough of them that she couldn't miss the flashing red shield at the bottom of the monitor. "What's that?" she asked, pointing to it.

"Some kind of alert I haven't been able to diagnose. This is a hand-me-down system from a donor, and I'd say we got what we paid for."

"When I get some time later on, I'll take a look at it. Maybe it's just a matter of finding the explanation online and downloading a program that will fix it once and for all."

"If you can get this thing running properly, I'll owe you big-time."

"Just part of the job, boss," Bekah told her with a grin. "We all do what we can, right?"

That got her a short laugh. "That's one of Drew's favorite lines. I think you've been spending too much time with that troublemaker."

"Troublemaker? What do you mean?"

"He's one of those love 'em and leave 'em types, and he's left a string of broken hearts from here to Louisville. He's a good enough guy, but he just can't seem to settle down."

Bekah knew perfectly well that Drew's romantic exploits were none of her business, but her curiosity got the better of her. "Why do you think that is?"

After considering the question for a moment, she replied, "Either he's looking for something particular that he can't find, or he's got no clue what he wants and is hoping to blindly run into it somewhere along the way."

"Or he's happy being unattached," Bekah suggested. "Some guys like having the freedom to wander from one woman to the next whenever they get bored."

She'd known more than her share of them, she added silently. Men who told a woman what she wanted to hear, then shed her when things got too serious or she asked too many questions that he didn't want to answer. Either way, he broke away cleanly and got on with his life, while she was left behind, wondering what had gone wrong.

"It's like Erin always says. Boys are stupid."

"You mean Drew's sister?" When Sierra nodded, Bekah couldn't help laughing. "With those three as brothers, I guess she oughta know."

"Got that right. So, our new tenant is a dehydrated squirrel with a broken leg. Are you ready for your first lesson in squirrel care?"

"That depends. What's the medical term for a broken leg?" She'd watched enough medical dramas to have a decent idea what the answer was, so she figured it wouldn't be too hard for the struggling vet tech to come up with something reasonable.

"Ugh, not now."

"Yes, now," Bekah insisted. "Come on, you must know at least one of the words."

"The upper bone in a leg is the femur."

"And?"

Sierra stared up, as if she might find a clue written on the water-stained ceiling tiles. Then she snapped her fingers and gave Bekah a delighted smile. "Fractured."

"Let's see if you're right." Tapping the phrase into the search box on the computer, she angled the screen so her new friend could see that she was right. "Nice job."

"Great," Sierra muttered with a wry grin. "One down, forty-million to go."

"One step at a time," Bekah reminded her. "No matter how big or small a project is, that's how everything gets done."

Sierra studied her for a long moment, then smiled. "Forget Lily. I think I just found my new tutor. How much do you want?"

Stunned by the request, she firmly shook her head. "Me? I'm not a teacher."

"Teachers help their students learn, and you just did that perfectly. I can't afford the time or money to retake classes, which means I have to pass on the first go-round. So, are you going to name a price or make me come up with one on my own?"

Bekah didn't have the first idea what that kind of job should pay, but the humming laptop inspired her. "Why don't I look up what private tutors normally make, and then we can talk?"

"Deal." After they shook hands, she said, "Now, come with me and I'll show you how to examine our little acorn-loving rodent without getting bit."

Not a completely even trade, Bekah decided as she followed her quirky new boss, but it was definitely a start.

At lunchtime, Bekah finally convinced Mrs. Kinley to let her help clean up the kitchen. "But you really have to call me Maggie," she'd insisted with a bright, dimpled smile. "Everyone else does."

That didn't seem right to Bekah, so while they worked she simply avoided calling Drew's mother anything at all. Unfortunately, the woman was pretty perceptive, and she laughed. "Just give in and go with it, honey. We're all pretty casual around here, which you'll find out soon enough."

"It's true," Lily chimed in while she dried one of the large platters and put it away. "It sounds corny, but around here we're one big, crazy family."

It didn't sound corny to Bekah at all. In fact, she'd felt more at home in the Kinleys' loud, chaotic house than she had anywhere else in recent memory. She really appreciated them including her in their homey routine and offering her a place to sleep that didn't include seat belt connectors jabbing her in the back. She wasn't sure how to say that without it coming across as lame, so she kept the comment to herself. Instead, she said, "I like big, crazy families. There's always room for someone new."

"Around here, that's definitely the case," Lily agreed, sending a smile over to her husband, who was currently arguing with Drew about something farm-related. "When I first started coming by for riding lessons, I felt like one of the crew right off the bat."

"Coming up with that riding school idea for you and Mike didn't hurt any," Maggie reminded her with a fond look. "It's still bringing kids in here, and the money sure does come in handy."

"How about the rescue center?" Bekah asked while she rinsed dishes and lined them up in the dishwasher. "From what Sierra was saying, I got the feeling it runs pretty close to the bone."

"And then some," Drew answered as he swung onto a stool in front of the large island. "We'd all like to step back and let it earn its own way, but it's gotta prove it can turn a profit first. We don't have the money to hire full-time staff—"

"But it can't support itself without them," Bekah finished for him.

She almost expected him to scold her for interrupting, but instead he nodded. "Right. Sounds to me like you've got a pretty good head for business."

"I wish," she replied with a derisive laugh. "Mostly, I understand flat-line finances."

Moving a little closer, he eyed his mother before replying in a quieter voice obviously meant to spare her feelings. "Yeah, same with us. We've been tread-ing water since my father died a few years ago. Mike came back to help out, and his wedding carriage busi-ness and riding school are helping to keep us out of bankruptcy, but it's not fun, that's for sure."

"Especially since the rescue center isn't pulling its weight. If you have to close it, what will happen to all those animals? Is there another facility like that around here somewhere?"

"Not for wildlife. Dogs and cats, they're easy. Lots of folks will adopt an animal from a shelter as long as it's healthy. Raccoons and deer that need attention from a vet, they're a different story."

"And hawks," Bekah added, swallowing around a sudden lump in her throat. "If it wasn't for Sierra, Rosie would've died yesterday."

"That'd be a shame. I'm looking forward to watch-ing her fly again."

His hazel eyes twinkled with anticipation, and Bekah felt the barricade she'd built around herself start to wobble. She didn't know how he'd done it, but this outgoing, bighearted country boy had somehow edged around her defenses and begun earning her trust. Out of harsh necessity, she didn't give it easily, so her re-action to him was baffling, to say the least.

When the kitchen was back in order, he hopped down from the stool and angled her toward the door. "Come on. I've got something to show you."

"I should get back to the center and make sure ev-eryone's okay. Sierra has to make a presentation in class tonight, so she left to polish her slide show."

"A few more minutes won't matter," he assured her with a bright grin as he opened the door for her. "If you get in trouble, just tell her it was my fault. She'll believe that."

Mischief glinted in his eyes, and she couldn't help laughing. "Okay, but it has to be quick."

"Yes, ma'am."

She couldn't imagine what he had in mind, and she was surprised when he headed for the well-worn field road that led to the center. Instead of going in the front door of the clinic, he took her around back and paused by a door that looked as though it hadn't been used in years. Oddly, the glass set into the weathered oak had been freshly cleaned, and new curtains hung across the window next to the door.

Drew dug into the pocket of his jeans and pulled out a dull brass key, which he promptly held out to her.

Stunned by the implication, she reflexively shook her head and started backpedaling. "What did you do?"

"You need a place to stay," he replied in a reasonable tone. "We need a night manager for this place. It's a win-win."

She couldn't deny that, for her, the solution was ideal. Buried here on this farm in the middle of nowhere, she'd be impossible for anyone to find, even if they knew where to look. Beyond that, she already loved working at the center, caring for the animals who needed a little boost to get healthy enough to be adopted or returned to where they belonged.

Having been injured and grounded in her own way, Bekah felt a special kinship with the creatures who were biding their time until they were strong enough to be back on their own.

While she debated with herself, she noticed Drew watching her closely. *He must think I'm a complete loon*, she groaned silently. Hoping to prove him wrong, she shook off her reservations and summoned a grateful smile. "Is this where you've been disappearing to lately?"

"Yeah."

"And getting scolded for skipping work at the farm?"

"Actually," he confided with a charmingly crooked grin, "it wasn't that bad. Mike growls a lot, but ever since he married Lily, he's more teddy bear than grizzly."

She doubted that, but it was nice of him to downplay the scolding he must have gotten from his older brother on her account. She couldn't remember anyone ever going out on a limb like that for her, and his thoughtfulness touched her in a way that she hadn't felt in ages. Since he'd gone to so much trouble for her, she figured the least she could do was view the result of his hard work. "Well, let's see how it looks, and then we'll go from there."

He didn't take the key from her or muscle past her to do the manly open-the-door routine. Instead, he let her unlock the old knob and enter the small space on her own. When it occurred to her that he intended to wait outside, she turned to him and asked, "Are you coming in?"

"Only if you like it."

For all those rugged looks of his, he was a real sweetheart. The seeming contradiction actually suited him pretty well, she thought with a smile. Not to mention, it made him even more appealing to her. It seemed that there was more to this country boy than a quick smile and an easygoing personality. Despite her plan to keep some distance between them, she couldn't help wondering just how much there was to discover about him.

She left the door open in a silent invitation, then walked into what appeared to be an old office with a small bathroom at the back. Although it was connected to the baby barn by a short walkway, the separate entrance offered some privacy, and the thick wall blocked out most of the noise. None of the furnishings were new, but the bedding and curtains looked freshly laundered, and a vintage refrigerator was humming away in the corner of the tiny kitchen.

For several seconds, she wasn't sure how to react. When she realized he must be waiting for her to respond somehow, she said, "This is incredible."

"You might want to hold your applause till I show you this." He strode to the small kitchen sink, turned the cold handle and waited.

And waited.

After about ten seconds, a horrible moaning kicked in somewhere behind the wall, traveling up the pipes and into the faucet. As if that wasn't disheartening enough, it was followed by a rust-colored trickle of water from the tap. The pressure gradually increased, and the water began flowing at a more normal rate.

"The bathroom fixtures aren't any better right now, I'm afraid," he told her. "I know it looks bad, but the water's been off for a long time. I'm sure it'll clear up soon. I ordered a new toilet, and Mom said you're welcome to shower at the house until things are okay in here."

Doing a slow pivot to take it all in, she stopped when she came around to Drew. "You did all this for me?"

"Well, cleaning's not my favorite chore, but once I got started, it didn't make sense to quit until everything was decent for you." He gave her another one of those charming grins that he seemed to have quite a collection of. "Gotta admit I'm a little jealous. Your place is cleaner than mine."

"I'm confused," she confided with a frown. "Why would you go to so much trouble for someone you just met yesterday?"

"It seems like you need a place to land, and I wanted to give you one."

"Why do you care?"

He started to answer, then grimaced and sighed. "I'm really not sure. It just felt like the right thing to do."

"Do you always follow your gut like that?"

"Pretty much."

That had never worked out well for her, so she'd stopped doing it long ago. But now, standing here with this man who'd taken it upon himself to help her, she was beginning to wonder if the problem wasn't with her, after all. Maybe, she thought for the first time, it was the fault of the people who'd disappointed her so badly.

While she mulled that over, she noticed that he wasn't trying to pressure her into gushing about his generosity, or even accepting it. Instead, he gazed at her with a patient expression that was simply amazing to someone who'd been pushed, goaded and manipulated into doing far too many things she should've had the good sense to refuse.

And because he was allowing her to choose for herself, her decision was an easy one.

"Thank you, Drew," she finally said, smiling up at him in gratitude. "You did a great job, and I think I'll be very comfortable living here."

By the time Drew had finished the chores that had been piling up and showed his face in the hay barn that afternoon, Mike and Josh had stacked more than half of the small bales waiting to be tucked away in the overhead lofts.

"I know," Drew said, stalling the expected dressing-down with both hands in the air. "I'll work extra time tonight to make it up."

His brothers exchanged a very male look and then, to his astonishment, started laughing like maniacs.

"Did I miss something?" Drew asked, perplexed by their attitude. Normally, going AWOL for hours on end was an invitation to a very unpleasant big-brother scolding, complete with folded arms and a heavy dose of scowls. For some reason, today it was hilarious.

"Josh," Mike began, pointedly ignoring Drew, "when's the last time you heard of Drew putting off one backbreaking job to take on another, even dirtier backbreaking job?"

"Well, now, let me see," the youngest Kinley drawled, tapping his chin with a leather-gloved finger. When he was done stalling, he grinned at Drew. "I'm thinkin' never. Then again, he didn't meet Bekah till this week."

"Very funny," Drew grumbled. "Can we get to work now?"

Mike laughed at that. "Not just yet, Romeo. My wife pointed out something about Bekah after dinner last night, and I wanna run it past you."

Lily had an uncanny set of instincts when it came to people, so Drew couldn't resist hearing what his very intuitive sister-in-law had to say about Bekah. "Okay."

"That girl out there," he pointed in the general direction of the rescue center, "is running from something, and she needs a place to hide." Crossing his arms, he pegged Drew with a stern, head-of-the-family kind of look. "How'm I doing so far?"

"I totally agree, which is why I had Harley do a quick check on her in the sheriff's database. Nothing popped up."

"That's nuts," Josh muttered with a dark look. "Anyone with eyes can see someone hit her not long ago. You mean to tell me she didn't report it?"

"Some women never do," Mike replied in a somber voice. "They're afraid to make the guy even madder by getting the law involved."

"Who could do that to a sweet woman like her?" Josh demanded.

"I don't know," Drew replied. "But he better pray that he never meets up with me."

His brothers nodded in agreement, and he felt a rush of gratitude for their support. As Bekah had pointed out more than once, she was a stranger here in Oaks Crossing, and it would be easy for most folks to ignore what was right in front of their faces.

But not his family, Drew thought proudly. No matter how hard it might be for them, Kinleys always tried to do the right thing. In fact, he mused as he and Mike climbed into the hayloft, how hard something was usually told him that it was the right way to go. That was probably on a motivational plaque somewhere, but being a Kentucky farm boy, he'd learned it the way he learned most things.

The hard way.

Caught up in his mental wandering, he missed the bale that Josh tossed up to him, and it knocked him to the dusty floor near the edge of the hayloft. Glaring down at the wagon, he yelled, "Hey!"

"Sorry, man. You were lookin' right at me, so I figured you were ready."

They began to argue about what being "ready" to catch a seventy-pound bale of hay looked like, and Mike stepped in to restore some peace. "Drew, if you're lost in space, take the rest of the day off and come back tomorrow. If you fall over the side and break your neck, Mom'll kill me."

"I'm fine," Drew insisted stubbornly. "Josh caught me by surprise is all."

That started another round of arguing, and finally Mike ended it. "Enough!"

Even though they were all grown up now, he and Josh never messed with their big brother when he yelled like that. It was his end-of-my-rope bellow, and he only hauled it out when he meant business. After a deep breath to cool a temper that could still be as bad as it had ever been, Mike ordered Josh to head back out to bale one more wagonload of hay and bring it in before dark.

When he was gone, Mike turned to Drew with a disgusted look. "You two have to figure out how to get along better. You're driving me insane."

"It's his fault for being such a pain."

"I'm gonna tell you what Dad used to tell me when

I said that about you," Mike shot back. "You're older, and you should know better."

"Aw, come on," Drew whined. "I can't help that I was born two years earlier than him."

"If he was the older one, I'd be having this pointless conversation with him. Now, get down there and start tossing that hay up here before I send you out to dig ditches or something."

"You're all heart, big brother." Grinning, Drew jumped from the loft down onto the top layer of hay. They'd been doing this kind of work most of their lives, and they quickly got into a rhythm that whittled down the wagonload and started filling in the blank spaces in the storage area above.

After they'd been at it for a while, they took a break for some water. Sitting on a bale down below, Drew looked up at his twice-married brother, who sat with his battered cowboy boots dangling over the loft's edge. "Can I ask you something?"

"Shoot."

"How did you go from being divorced and 'never gonna get married again' to proposing to Lily?"

"Faith."

The answer came without hesitation, and Drew cocked his head in disbelief. "In what?"

"Oh, not mine," he amended with a chuckle. "Lily's. She saw past all my nonsense to who I really am and somehow liked what she found. The rest is a mystery to me, but it seems to work."

"So, you're saying you have no idea what changed your mind."

"Pretty much." After a swig of water, he added,

"But I have to say, if it could happen to a jaded guy like me, it could probably happen to anyone."

Drew had to admit, he had a point there. He'd lived his entire life in Oaks Crossing, so he hadn't been kicked around by the world the way Mike had. But even though he'd had plenty of girlfriends and one near-miss in the down-the-aisle department, none of them had stuck. He was still baffled about why that was, especially since he dated sweet, uncomplicated women who'd gone on to marry one friend or another of his over the years.

Was the problem with them, or him?

This was one of those times that he really missed talking with his father. Dad had a knack for taking any problem and distilling it down into its most basic elements so he could help Drew figure out what to do.

"Go ahead," Mike nudged quietly. "Ask me."

Drew hesitated, then decided there was no harm in posing the question. "I'm really not all that picky. Why can't I find what I'm looking for?"

"Who says you haven't?"

Mike gave him a knowing look, and Drew groaned. "You can't be serious. I just met Bekah."

"What makes you think I was talking about Bekah?" When Drew glared at him, he grinned. "I could've been referring to any of the girls you've known, but you went right to her. What you have to ask yourself is, why?"

With that, Mike climbed to his feet, effectively declaring their philosophy lesson over. While they finished this load and Josh towed in the last one of the day, Drew had very little time to think about anything else.

To his mind, he was better off that way.

When they were finished, he realized his truck was still parked at his house.

"Stay with us tonight," Mike suggested. "Mom won't mind."

Ordinarily, Drew would prefer to be in his own bed, but he was too tired to argue. "Okay, thanks." He'd just finished speaking when his cell phone kicked out a classic-rock ringtone that made him grin. "It's Nolan Parks. I haven't talked to him in ages. Wonder what's up."

"Tell him hey from us," Josh said as he strolled out to his pickup and Mike headed inside.

"Will do." Drew clicked his phone on and said, "I haven't heard from you since you moved to Denver. How're things going?" In reply, he got an earful of excited chatter that reminded him of his niece. "Whoa, man, slow down. You sound like a Smurf."

Nolan took a breath and asked, "Did you check your email yet?"

"I'm still at the farm, so no. Why?"

"Just do it. I'll wait."

Must be important, Drew thought, putting the phone on speaker while he accessed his mailbox. When he opened the message his old buddy was so jazzed about, he skimmed it with growing enthusiasm. "You want me to be a partner in your ecotourism business?"

"Yeah. Silver Creek Wilderness Adventures is growing like crazy, and I've got more clients than I can handle on my own. So I thought of you. Check out the photos I sent you."

Only half listening to Nolan's running commentary, Drew clicked through a dozen pictures, each more stunning than the last. The final one was a sunset shot from the top of a small mountain, with nothing in sight but trees and an outcrop dusted with snow. Having grown up surrounded by some of Kentucky's finest scenery, he was used to rolling hills and wide-open spaces. But the sprawling wilderness he was seeing now took his breath away.

"That's incredible," he said with humble appreciation for God's high-altitude handiwork. "Where is it?"

"In my backyard," Nolan replied proudly. "My cabin's about a quarter mile to the west of what you're looking at. It's got two bedrooms, both with a view just like this."

"How much land do you own?" Drew asked while he continued surfing through the pictures.

"Fifty acres, give or take, depending on how high the river's running," he clarified with a chuckle. "I take folks hiking, canoeing, kayaking, wilderness camping, whatever they want to try while they're here. I'm thinking about adding horseback-riding tours in the spring, so naturally I thought of you."

"You're sure you don't want Mike for that?"

"Not a chance." Nolan snorted. "That control freak and I would kill each other in a week."

The question had been moot, anyway, since Mike wasn't about to uproot his family and move across the country. While they continued discussing Nolan's fast-growing company, Drew was flattered to be considered for something more than what he often described as infantry work. He'd be a full partner in the business, and while the sum Nolan named as his buy-in wasn't small, Drew had the money he would need tucked away in the bank, waiting for something important to come along.

This could be it, he thought, his enthusiasm for the idea escalating while they talked. He'd always wanted to do something like this, and not only would he be co-owner and trail boss, he'd finally get his chance to break free from his tiny hometown and experience something beyond the county line. He was beginning to understand Kelly's motivation for leaving him behind and heading for the West Coast. Nice as Oaks Crossing was, it didn't have much in the way of opportunities for expanding your horizons.

Then reality came crashing in, and his excitement dimmed. His family relied on his various skills around the farm, and much as he'd love to strike out on his own, it was more complicated than that. Dad and Granddad had put everything they had into making Gallimore Stables a success, and these days he, Mike and Josh were doing the same. It took all of them, from sunup to sundown, to keep the farm above water, and right now there was no way they could manage to pay the going rate for outside help.

Maybe next year, Drew mused, then quickly dashed his own hopes. The economy wouldn't be any better then, and there wouldn't be any fewer horses or acres to care for. Not to mention, every building they owned would be another year older, on the brink of another round of do-or-die maintenance they couldn't afford to hire out.

While his mind grappled with the options, his gut was telling him that if he didn't make a move now, he never would. This decision was the biggest he'd ever faced, and while instinct was telling him to go for it, loyalty to his family made him hesitate. "I really appreciate the offer, but this would be a huge step for me. Can you give me some time to think it over?"

Silence crackled on the line, and he thought he might have lost the connection. Then Nolan came back on with a drawn-out, "Sure, I guess. I gotta admit, with the way you've always talked about seeing the world someday, I thought you'd snap this up and book yourself on the red-eye to Denver tonight. Is everything okay there?"

That was a loaded question, and Drew artfully sidestepped it. "Just a few things to work through."

"Okay, but I need an answer soon. Out here, this is the best time of year to buy horses, 'cause folks don't wanna stable them over the winter. You ever ride a snowmobile?"

"In Kentucky?" he scoffed. "Not hardly."

"We'll change that real fast. Call me at this number as soon as you make a decision. We've got a lot of details to iron out."

"You're talking like I've already signed on."

"Positive thinking, buddy," Nolan replied with a chuckle. "It's gotten me this far, and I'm sticking with it until it quits working."

They said goodbye, and Drew hung up, staring at his phone screen until it went black. Tempted beyond reason by Nolan's unexpected offer, he gazed up into a dark sky dotted with stars. From the barn behind him, he heard a quiet nicker and the shuffling of hooves as a couple of horses moved around in their stalls. Crickets and frogs chimed in with their routine nighttime chorus, accented by the yip of a coyote off in the distance.

Familiar and comfortable, those sounds represented the life he'd always known. Did he want to hang on to them? he wondered as he trudged up the back-porch steps. Or did he want to open himself up to the possibility of something else?

The choice was simple enough: stay or go. But he recognized that he was too exhausted to make such an important decision tonight. He was impulsive by nature, so the delay didn't sit well with him, and he prayed that putting it off wouldn't turn out to be a worse mistake than jumping in too quickly.

Chapter Four

The next day, it was still dark when Bekah walked up the lane that led to the Kinley farmhouse. There were a few muted lights on inside, so she moved quietly toward the kitchen door, which was unlocked just like Drew had told her it always was. Bekah couldn't recall ever living in a place where people didn't use locks, dead bolts and alarms to keep their homes safe. Quiet little Oaks Crossing was about as far from those rough city blocks as she could possibly get.

When she stepped inside, she tiptoed through the huge kitchen and back hallway to the bathroom Maggie had generously offered to let her use. When she came out, she stopped abruptly when she noticed what was seated at the breakfast bar. Or rather, who she saw there, slurping cereal from a bowl while pawing through an actual printed newspaper.

Seeing her in the dim light, Drew grinned and saluted her with his spoon. "Morning."

"Good morning." Clutching her backpack tighter for some reason, she recovered enough of her wits to register that he was wearing the same jeans and T-shirt he'd been in when she last saw him yesterday. "Did you sleep here?"

"Yeah," he replied with a yawn. "By the time we got done with everything, it was almost ten, so I crashed on the couch. How was your night?"

"I haven't slept this well in weeks," she answered truthfully. "It's so peaceful here, I dropped right off and didn't move till that old alarm clock woke me."

"I'm glad to hear that. Sometimes settling in to a new place can be rough."

He had no idea, she thought bitterly. Catching herself headed down the same path that had led her to no end of trouble, she shook off the gloomy mood with determination. Those days were behind her, and she'd been granted an opportunity to leave them a distant memory. Somehow, she'd find a way to make things different for herself.

Because quite honestly, she didn't have a choice.

Then she heard herself ask, "Would you like some eggs?"

"Don't tell me you cook, too," he teased, giving her that charmingly crooked grin that had put her at ease during their difficult first meeting.

"I'm not exactly a gourmet, but I can crack open an egg and make it edible." Setting her bag on the floor, she opened a fridge whose contents rivaled some small markets she'd shopped in. She glanced over her shoulder and said, "Your mother's got everything in here. What would you say to a Western omelet?"

"Howdy?"

This grin had a mischievous quality, and she laughed. "Very funny. I meant, would you like one?"

"Sure, but only if you show me how to make one.

That way, I won't be totally helpless in the kitchen anymore."

She had a hard time envisioning this tall, capable man being helpless anywhere he might find himself, but the idea of them cooking together appealed to her for some reason. Even if it was only a simple breakfast. "Okay, but I'm in charge, so you have to listen."

Where had that come from? she wondered, shocked by the teasing note she heard in her voice. Out of lifelong habit, she was normally a very serious person. The only explanation she could think of for the lapse was that Drew's lighthearted nature was contagious.

"Yes, ma'am," he promised, though the smirk he was wearing made her wonder if he meant it. She'd find out soon enough, she decided while she handed ingredients to him.

His comedy routine continued, as each time she picked something up, he narrated what it was and what she did with it. Not only was it entertaining, his running commentary helped make her feel more at ease in his mother's kitchen. By the time they'd settled down to eat, Bekah realized she couldn't have asked for a better start to her day than sharing breakfast with Drew Kinley.

"Water should be better at your place today," he told her after swallowing a mouthful of omelet. "If not, let me know, and I'll call a buddy of mine who's a plumber and owes me a favor."

"Meaning he won't charge me for the repairs?" Drew nodded, and she smiled. "I really appreciate you doing that."

"No problem. It's the least I can do to repay you for

the breakfast. Usually, I wolf down a couple of bagels or muffins on my way here."

"Because you're late?"

That made him chuckle. "Pretty much. Mike and Josh don't have a problem getting themselves in gear so early, but I've never been much of a morning person."

"I thought that was a requirement for people growing up on a farm."

"It is. It's just not me."

He sipped his coffee, and she wondered if she should voice the question that had popped into her head all of a sudden. Then again, he knew plenty about her already, so she mustered up the courage to ask, "What *is* you?"

"I'm not sure, but I've always believed God had something different in mind for me than this."

Having drifted from place to place for most of her life, Bekah had never been part of any community long enough to get any kind of religious education. She vaguely remembered some of the Bible stories her late grandmother had read to her as a child, but other than that, she didn't have an even passing acquaintance with the Almighty. Hearing Drew speak about Him so easily made her wonder if she'd been missing something.

That was a topic for another time, so she put it out of her mind and refocused on their conversation. "Then why do you stay here?"

"Don't get me wrong—I like the work well enough. And I love my brothers, even though they drive me nuts on a daily basis."

"That's only fair—" Lily's voice floated over from the doorway "—since they feel the same way about you."

Drew laughed, and Bekah slid her stool down to make room for Lily. "Would you like some eggs?"

"Absolutely, but I'll take them scrambled. Thank you." Pouring herself a glass of orange juice, she looked over at Drew. "I should warn you, Mike's got a long list of jobs for you today. Something about making up for lost time."

"Yeah, yeah, yeah. What else is new?"

Footsteps creaked on the oak staircase, and Mike joined the group huddled around the breakfast dishes. He poured them each another cup of coffee and cocked his head with male interest. "Is that ham and peppers I smell?"

So, since she was the one holding the spatula, Bekah whipped up eggs for Lily and a farmer's omelet stuffed with ham, cheese and peppers for Mike. A pudgy golden retriever that Mike called Charlie and a scruffy terrier who answered to the name Sarge ambled in from the living room, sniffing the air with canine interest. By the time Maggie and Abby joined them, Lily had fed the dogs, the humans had shifted over to the large dining table, and Bekah was moving around the big kitchen like she'd been living on the farm for years.

It was the kind of wonderful homey feeling she'd always longed for but had never known how to create. That she'd found it here, in this tiny town so far from the world she knew, was difficult to believe.

But no matter how many times she pinched herself, the image didn't change. She still wasn't sure what might happen to her in the future, but she'd always be grateful for the odd circumstances that had brought her to Oaks Crossing.

* * *

One night as he was driving home from the farm, Drew noticed lights on in the clinic. It was long past closing time, and the only car in the parking lot was Bekah's sad-looking hatchback with its ruined windshield. He'd be amazed if the engine even started after sitting idle for so long. Accustomed to being on the go every day, he couldn't imagine being stranded in one place that way.

Bekah seemed content to spend all her time on the farm, either at the clinic or with the family. Drew had gotten the feeling that her reluctance to mingle with anyone else was a clue about her very hazy background, but she hadn't offered any more details about herself lately. Her personal history must be so painful that she didn't want to think about it. The idea of her struggling through that kind of trouble on her own still made him angry, and as he got out of his pickup, he resolved to unravel the mystery of her someday. No matter how long it took.

When he tried the handle on the front door, he was pleased to find it locked. Bekah was scowling at the old laptop on the counter, and when she heard the rattle, her head whipped up to reveal a look of all-out panic on her pretty face. More than startled, she looked terrified.

Feeling bad for scaring her, he forced a reassuring smile and waved at her. She seemed rooted in place, and they stood there for several moments, staring at each other. It was the epitome of how their new friendship had been going, he realized: he trying to get in, she shutting him out.

Finally, she seemed to decide it was okay to let

him into the lobby and came over to twist open the sturdy lock.

"You took ten years off my life," she scolded, fastening the bolt behind him. "What are you doing here this time of night?"

"Sorry to scare you, but I was on my way home and saw the lights on. Is everything okay?"

"The animals are fine, but our system—" she flung a frustrated hand toward the computer "—is the sickest thing in the building."

Drew noticed she called it "our system," and he liked knowing that she included herself as one of the full-time staff. Even if there were currently only two of them. "Anything I can do?"

"Can you fix a computer?"

"Well, no, but I could distract you for a while. Maybe if you give it a rest and focus on something else, the solution will come to you."

"So you've come to save the damsel in distress from the electronic dragon?"

She'd struck him as being a very somber person, so the unexpected fairy-tale reference made him grin. "More or less."

"My hero. What did you have in mind?"

"I'm starving. How 'bout dinner? I hear the Oaks Café just put in a whole new menu I haven't tried yet."

"Is that the place that's been doing renovations?" she asked.

"Yeah. Why?"

Suddenly, she looked very uncertain. Casting a look toward the back of the building, she nibbled her lower lip as if she was considering something that impacted the fate of her world. When she came back to him, some of the worry had left her features, but too much was left behind for his taste. He couldn't imagine what was bothering her, but his gut told him that if he pushed, she'd clam up and refuse to tell him anything.

So he waited.

After several more seconds, she finally confided, "Sierra mentioned they have a new Laundromat attached to the restaurant."

"Cool idea, huh?"

"Is it finished?"

"I think so." Then it hit him why she was more interested in the laundry facilities than in having dinner with him. "I'm guessing you're out of clean clothes."

"Tomorrow is it. I was going to do them here, but Sierra nixed that idea."

"Aw, man," he groaned. "That'd be gross. Why didn't you just ask Mom?"

"I really hate to impose any more than I already have. I mean, it was bad enough to take over Abby's room that way, but your mom constantly invites me up there for meals. And she insists I call her 'Maggie.'"

"No," Drew exclaimed on a mock gasp. "What is that woman thinking?"

"I know it sounds dumb to you, but I've learned that no matter how nice people might be, it doesn't take long to overstay my welcome."

The soft confession blew away any thought of teasing her further, and Drew fought the urge to take her in his arms and reassure her that her fears were completely unfounded. Instead, he met her worried gaze with a smile. "I don't know how they do things in Chicago, but around here, folks don't have a time limit on hospitality. You've done more than pull your weight ever since you got here, and we're happy to have you."

"For now, anyway."

That kind of pessimism was a learned trait, and it pained him to know that this bright, beautiful woman had picked it up somewhere along what must have been a difficult path. Since he couldn't unlearn it for her, he figured the best thing he could do was prove to her that there was another way to go. And then show her how to get there herself.

"I'm still starving," he said briskly, stepping back to give her some space. "And I'm gonna try out the new menu at the Oaks. Wanna come?"

She hesitated, then asked, "Do you mind if I do laundry while we're there?"

"'Course not. I'll even help you fold."

She rewarded him with a warm, grateful smile. "Are you still trying to be my hero?"

Yes, Drew nearly blurted before he caught himself and dialed his reaction back a notch. "Maybe."

For the first time since he'd met her, Bekah let out a real, heartfelt laugh rather than the contained one he'd heard until now. In keeping with his new gallant status, he waited while she locked the clinic door and then followed her to her apartment. She jammed her clothing into her oversize duffel, and before she could lift it, he hefted it to his shoulder and motioned her out the door. "After you."

"Is this the Southern gentleman thing I've always read about?" she asked as she locked the door and followed him out to his truck.

"Yes, ma'am," he drawled with a grin. "We don't

just haul out these manners to impress the tourists, y'know."

"I'll keep that in mind."

Drew hadn't met many people who'd grown up anywhere other than Kentucky, and the differences between his upbringing and Bekah's fascinated him. During their ride into town, they traded details about where they'd lived, and he learned that while Bekah had a fondness for Chicago, she and her family actually hadn't been there all that long. Being born and raised on the rolling acreage of Gallimore Stables, he couldn't help wondering what he'd be like if he'd had the opportunity to experience new cities and people the way she had.

While he pondered how to keep their intriguing conversation going, she looked out the passenger window with a heavy sigh. "Most places I've lived, it's never really dark like this. There are so many street lights, you can't even see the stars. And you can hardly sleep through the traffic noise, much less hear the birds."

"Cities have parks, though."

"Sure, but this whole area is like one enormous park," she commented in a dreamy voice. "With all the horses and wild animals around, it goes on and on, with nothing to ruin the beauty of it."

Drew had always considered his hometown to be a pretty place, but Bekah made it sound like paradise. Then again, that was probably because she'd had such a rough time lately and appreciated the tranquillity Oaks Crossing had to offer. Since he'd had more than his fill of peace and quiet, he longed for something more exciting. Images of Nolan's Silver Creek property in

Colorado floated through his mind, but he resolutely pushed them aside for another time.

When they arrived in town, it was about eight o'clock, and the sidewalks had been rolled up for the night. The vintage-style street lights were on their lowest setting, so that anyone out for a stroll wouldn't stumble, and the upper end of Main Street had a see-you-in-the-morning kind of vibe.

At the other end, though, shining like a beacon of modern-day convenience, stood the newly refurbished Oaks Café. The small porch was full of rocking chairs and hanging baskets of flowers that reminded him of the old homes populating the town. With large front windows and strains of modern country music pouring through the open front doors, it seemed to invite anyone who was still around to come in and stay a while.

Standing near the door, Drew found an old friend he hadn't seen in at least ten years. "Cam Stewart?" he exclaimed in surprise as they traded an enthusiastic hug. "What are you doing in town? You said the only way you'd ever come back here was in a pine box."

"Yeah, well, Mom's last stroke changed my mind."

"I'm so sorry," Drew murmured. "I heard she was doing better."

"You heard wrong."

No mention of the details, and no invitation to ask about them, Drew noticed. Taking the hint, he turned to Bekah. "Bekah Holloway, this is Cam, the black sheep of the Stewart family."

"Pleased to meet you," she said, ducking her head as they shook hands. In the past few days, Drew had decided she wasn't necessarily shy but definitely avoided making eye contact with new acquaintances. It didn't take a genius to figure out she was trying desperately to keep people from remembering her face.

But why?

All the reasons he'd come up with were bad, so he put the question out of his mind for now and forged ahead. Keenly aware of Bekah's discomfort, he said, "I see the Laundromat's open for business. I don't suppose you've got any tables in there?"

"Sure, we do," Cam retorted as if the question was the most ridiculous thing he'd ever heard. "Folks need something to do while they're waiting for their loads to finish. It's mostly young people who do their laundry that way, and I thought if they had a chance to grab something to eat and chat with the other customers, it'd be more of a social thing than a chore."

"You always were the smart one."

"Speaking of smart," Cam said, glancing around to make sure no one was listening to them. "I hear Mike married a teacher. How'd a cranky old hound like him manage that one?"

"It's a mystery, that's for sure."

A young man who looked barely old enough to drive alone at night appeared outside the swinging doors that led to the back of the diner, waving his arms at Cam in a frantic gesture. Frowning, the diner's new manager patted Drew's shoulder on his way to put out whatever fire had erupted in the kitchen. "You go on in and find a seat. Menus are on the tables."

"Thanks."

Hefting the bag on to his shoulder, he noticed Bekah was sticking close to his side as they walked through the dining room to the laundry facilities. He'd like to think she was cozying up to him out of fondness, but he knew better. Being so much bigger than her, he made the ideal shield for her to hide behind until they were through the dining room and in the less crowded snack bar.

They were the only people with laundry, so they commandeered three washing machines and loaded them up. Dangling the empty bag from one strap, Drew chuckled. "How'd you get all that—" he nodded at the chugging machines "—in here?"

"Practice."

Her wry tone warned him not to pry any further, but once they'd ordered their dinners, he picked up the subject again.

"So," he began in the most disinterested voice he could manage, "wanna tell me why you're a packing savant?"

Shrugging, she sipped her ice water before responding. "Not really."

Strike one, Drew thought. Then again, he still had two more, so he gave it another shot. "Okay, so how'd a nice Chicago girl like you end up here in Oaks Crossing?"

Taking a handful of pretzels from the basket in the center of the table, she popped one in her mouth while she studied him closely. Drew had no idea what she might be looking for, but he endured her scrutiny with as much patience as he could muster. Normally, he wasn't one for playing games, but instinct told him that to Bekah, this was deadly serious. Maybe if he hung in there with her, he'd finally discover why.

After what felt like forever, she relented. "Let's just say I have a really bad sense of direction."

"Huh. Well, that's not much of an explanation."

"It's more of one than I've given anyone in a long time."

She added the kind of sad smile that only women seemed capable of delivering, and he was torn between pressing her for more and letting her be. Fortunately, their food arrived, giving him a chance to pull back far enough to let her breathe while they ate. The way she attacked her cheeseburger, it was as if she expected not to eat again for days.

"These waffle fries are fantastic," she said with an approving hum. "I wonder what's in this seasoning?"

"You could ask Cam, but knowing him, he'll probably look you dead in the eyes and say, 'I could tell you, but then I'd have to kill you.'"

That made her laugh, and he sensed her relaxing while they plowed through their meal. Drew suspected she'd never ask for anything else, so he took it upon himself to order more of the waffle fries for them to share.

When she was up shifting her clothes from washers to dryers, he flagged down their waitress and discreetly handed her his credit card. "This is on me, no matter what the lady says. Okay?"

"Sure. I'll run you a tab."

"Thanks."

"If you're interested, Wednesday is couples night in here. You get two-for-one if you bring in at least one load of laundry."

The concept reminded him of gas stations that offered a discount at the pumps if you washed your car in their bays. "That's a great idea. I had no clue Cam was such a business-oriented guy." Then he registered what she'd said, and he hurried to add, "But the lady and I are just friends."

"Every couple starts out that way, don't they?"

He couldn't dispute that, so he grinned. "I guess you're right."

Clearly pleased that she'd taught him something, she flounced back to the counter to place his order.

"Cute," Bekah commented when she rejoined him. "Flirting for tips."

The cynical assessment rubbed him the wrong way, and he frowned. "What makes you say that?"

"You really don't see it, do you?"

"See what?"

"How the women in this town stare at you when you walk by," she explained, dipping a fry into the puddle of ketchup she'd made on the plate. "With the way they all drool at the sight of you, you might as well be a piece of steak in the lion's pen at the zoo."

Drew was fairly certain she didn't realize that she'd just confessed to watching other women's reactions to him. Resting his elbows on the table, he leaned toward her with a grin. "Yeah? What else do they do?"

"Well, they—" She caught herself and gave him a scathing glare. "I'm not telling you. Your ego's big enough as it is."

"Really? What makes you say that?"

"Sierra told me."

Wonderful. He and the spunky vet tech student got along like brother and sister, which meant they'd had their share of run-ins and outright arguments. After talking to Sierra for about ten minutes when Erin first hired her, he'd realized that, despite his lady-killer reputation, they'd never be anything other than friends.

Why didn't he feel the same about Bekah? he wondered. There hadn't been an instant attraction on his end, but was that because she didn't appeal to him that way, or because she was so obviously vulnerable, and he didn't want her to think he was trying to take advantage of her precarious situation?

Or was it something else entirely?

Since he couldn't answer that, he set about repairing the tarnished image she had of him. But rather than tell her what a good guy he was, he devised a way for her to discover it for herself. "We've gotten to know each other a little since you got here. You really think I'm like that?"

"Well…" Clearly sifting through the interesting variety of experiences they'd shared, she eyed him warily, then shook her head. "I guess not. But Sierra knows you better than I do."

"I think you're smart enough to make up your own mind about lots of things," he said gently. "Including me."

Those gorgeous blue eyes widened in surprise, then narrowed with something much less attractive. "That's a line."

"No, it's not," he insisted quietly, edging closer so she'd be the only one to hear him. "Who was he, Bekah?"

"I don't know what you're talking about."

"The guy who scares you so much, you can't trust me not to hurt you the way he did."

Panic seized her features, and Drew was fairly certain that if he hadn't been parked between her and the door, she'd have bolted and never come back. When she seemed a bit calmer, he rested a comforting hand over hers. "You can be honest with me. I won't tell a soul, I promise."

Her free hand drifted to her cheek where that nasty bruise had finally faded but was clearly not forgotten. That told him that, although the wound was gone, she still felt the pain of it. Avoiding his gaze, she whispered, "It was a while ago. It's not important."

"It is to me."

When she met his eyes, hers shone with tears he suspected she'd been holding in for a long time. Blinking them away, she took a deep breath and started. "I was living in Cleveland, just barely scraping by. Then I got a temp job at the upscale department store where Richie works. We dated for a while, and then he asked me to move in. He promised he'd make everything better for me."

"But he didn't?"

"At first, he did," she explained in a halting voice. "But after a few months, I felt like he was smothering me. Following me to work, insisting I spend all my free time with him, even though he could leave me by myself and hang out with his friends whenever he felt like it. I didn't have any friends, and at one point it occurred to me that he wanted to keep it that way. Eventually, I told him I wanted to leave. But he wouldn't let me."

The last few words emerged in a strangled whisper, and he braced himself for tears. But they never came. Instead, she squared her shoulders and took a deep breath. "So that's my sad little story. Pathetic, huh?"

Tragic was the word Drew would have chosen, but he figured that if he shared his impression with her, she'd retreat back into herself and never tell him anything important again. The fact that she trusted him to keep her personal life to himself meant a lot to him. Because of his easygoing nature, most folks saw him as a big goof who didn't have much going on in the emotions department.

Bekah had called him her hero. He had every intention of proving to her that he was worthy of the title.

"I think the past belongs in the past," he said truthfully. "I admire anyone who can go through what you have and still keep going."

"You're just saying that. I'm nothing special."

That's where she was wrong, he thought, although he wasn't nearly ready to voice that opinion. So, rather than do something that might embarrass her further, he picked up the dessert menu and opened it to the sundaes. "So, vanilla or chocolate?"

"Strawberry."

"Strawberry it is." Flagging down the perky waitress, he ordered sundaes for each of them and something called the "topping carousel" that looked as if it contained every kind of ice cream garnish ever invented.

They chatted about lighter topics until their desserts arrived, then challenged each other to try various combinations of toppings until they were both laughing at the concoctions they came up with. It was crazy, but at one point it occurred to Drew that he hadn't had this much fun in months.

Since meeting Bekah that first eventful morning, every time he felt confident that he had her pegged, she surprised him again. He'd known his fair share of women, and while he liked all of them, none had captured his interest quite the way this one had. Slender but filled with a quiet inner strength he admired, she was by far the most fascinating woman he'd ever come across.

The trouble was, the last time he'd let himself start thinking this way, he'd ended up with a useless diamond ring and a broken heart. So, intriguing as she might be, Bekah Holloway would have to remain strictly off-limits for him. It was better for both of them.

Chapter Five

Bekah had never met a guy so willing to pitch in and lend a hand.

Whether the task was manual labor or folding clothes, it seemed to her that Drew was perfectly comfortable doing whatever needed to be done. By necessity, she'd gotten used to being on her own and taking care of everything herself. But now that there was someone around to shoulder some of the load for her, she had to admit she found having that kind of help comforting.

And a little unnerving. Because in her experience, when you started counting on someone, they held a power over your life you'd end up regretting. While it might be harder to manage on her own, in the long run it had always turned out for the best.

Until recently, she mused while she folded a pair of tattered jeans still warm from the dryer. The Kinleys— and Drew in particular—had gone out of their way to give her a measure of security and a place to call her own. Although she was grateful to them for their generosity, the skittish part of her still felt primed to run at a moment's notice.

Would she ever feel comfortable enough to settle somewhere? she wondered. The few days she'd spent in Oaks Crossing had made her yearn for something that lasted longer than a limited office assignment or a single growing season.

She wanted a home, she acknowledged with a mental sigh. The problem was, she didn't know how to make that happen.

"So," Drew said as he pulled another load from the dryer and dumped it in a wheeled basket. "What have you been able to do with the clinic's sick computer?"

"Nothing concrete. Every time I fix something and restart it, the diagnostics come up with something else. I'm hoping that if I just keep following the directions, eventually all the errors will be gone, and we can quit worrying about it."

That made him chuckle. "I don't know the first thing about those monsters. Where'd you learn about 'em?"

"Temp jobs, mostly. At one point, I worked in a factory where they had a system that kept acting up. It took me a while, but finally I zapped all the bugs, and it worked like a charm. The foreman was so thrilled, he gave me an afternoon off with pay."

"And what'd you do?"

"Laundry." Even to her ears that sounded pitiful, and she sighed. "Wow, I'm really boring."

He didn't contradict her, but he surprised her by asking, "What would you rather have done?"

Anything, she almost replied, then put the brakes on her cynicism before it could spoil the nice evening they'd been having. "I'm not sure. I was living in Baltimore at the time, so I could've gone to an Orioles game."

He rewarded her with a bright, country-boy grin. "That's what I would've done, for sure. Watching on TV is okay, but there's nothing like being there in person."

"When he had the money, my father used to take me to the Bears games on Sundays."

Horrified that she'd let such a personal detail slip out, she focused on the socks she was folding as if matching them up was the most crucial task she'd ever done.

Then, to her amazement, Drew said, "Before he died a few years ago, my dad used to take all of us to Cincinnati once a year for a Bengals game. He'd book connecting rooms at a nice hotel, so it was crazy expensive, but we always had a blast."

He didn't seem old enough to be mourning his father, and the nostalgic tone in his voice told her he missed a lot more than the annual football trip. Unaccustomed to dealing with other people's tragedies, she quietly said, "I'm so sorry you lost him."

"Thanks."

Suddenly, he seemed uncomfortable, and she searched for a way to shift to a less painful topic. Computers struck her as being fairly impersonal, so she went back to that. "Anyway, the laptop at the center is pretty new, so once I get all the nasties cleared off, it should work fine. Then Sierra can stop glaring at it all the time."

"You should ask her for an afternoon off," he suggested with a grin. "But don't do laundry."

She laughed, and then an idea she'd been toying with popped into the front of her mind. She hadn't mentioned it to anyone yet, and since Drew was being so nice, she thought it made sense to float it past him to see if it made sense to someone besides her. "Hey, can I get your opinion on something?"

Leaning back against an empty washer, he folded his arms with an expectant look. "Shoot."

"Well, I know the clinic is having a really hard time financially. Yesterday, Sierra told me that if she can't come up with a way to bring in more money, you're going to have to close it down at the end of the year. Have you guys ever thought of doing a fund-raiser to bring in some extra cash?"

"Not that I'm aware of. From what I've seen, she and the volunteers have their hands full just trying to take care of all the animals."

"That's what I was thinking, too," Bekah continued excitedly. "Now that I'm there to help out, we could come up with something unique that would draw people to the center for adoptions and admiring the wild-life we have there. Maybe we can tie it in with one of the animal releases that's coming up soon. We could give it a fun-sounding name, like Animal Palooza."

"Kinda like a zoo, but with critters you can take home."

He'd picked up on her train of thought without any effort at all, which ratcheted up her own enthusiasm for the idea several notches. "Right. What do you think?"

"It's a great idea, but local folks already know about the place, so you need to bring in people from farther away. In case you haven't noticed, Oaks Crossing is kind of off the map. How're you gonna get 'em here?"

"The same way you do with any other business. Advertising."

"Where?"

"Posters, flyers, the internet." Warming to the topic, she ticked the items off on her fingers. "Does the clinic have a website or media pages?"

That got her the blankest look she'd ever witnessed, and she laughed. "Never mind. I'll find out, and if we don't have them, I'll set them up. Most of that stuff is free, and you can reach tons of people with every post."

"You know how to do all that?"

"Not yet, but I will. The center is too important to let it go down without a fight." While she outlined her plan for learning what she needed, a smile crept across his tanned features until it warmed his eyes to a greenish-gold color even a skilled artist would be hard-pressed to capture. "What?"

"You're amazing, y'know that? You've been here a week, and already you've come up with a way to make life better for all those animals and the people who care so much about them."

"It's not that big a deal," she insisted, feeling self-conscious about the praise. "I just want to do something to help."

"I know," he murmured, his smile deepening to something she couldn't quite define. "That's what makes you amazing."

Because it was Drew, she knew he meant it. Smiling back, she felt the part of her that had been cowering in the shadows for so long take a tentative step back into the light.

And then, as if that wasn't enough, he offered her something she'd never consider asking him for. "A campaign like that sounds pretty ambitious for one person, so if you need a hand with anything, let me know. I can't do any of the technical stuff, but I've got a nice digital camera for taking pictures to use online or on flyers."

"You're a photographer?"

"I wouldn't go that far," he admitted with a chuckle, "but I love hiking and kayaking, and whenever I go fishing I usually come back with more cool nature shots than fish. Not to mention, the undeveloped land around the farm is a great place for taking pictures."

"I can imagine. I haven't gotten around to much of the area yet, but what I have seen is absolutely beautiful."

"Fall is pretty, but spring and summer are gorgeous. If you stick around long enough, you can see for yourself."

Was he asking her to stay? she wondered briefly before discarding the notion as ridiculous. She was hardly the type of woman a handsome, charming man like Drew Kinley would be interested in as more than a friend. Then again, there had been something unusual in the look he gave her when he told her she was amazing.

But she knew where those sorts of looks led, she reminded herself sternly. Nowhere good. Now that she was getting back on her own two feet, she had no intention of risking her newfound security by ceding even a slice of her life to anyone else.

Thanks to Richie, she'd suffered through enough romantic complications to last her a very long time. Maybe forever.

Saturday afternoon, Drew stopped by the clinic with his camera to get started on his new assignment as a wildlife photographer. After snapping a picture of the dainty fawn in the outside baby corral, Drew checked the viewfinder. She was cute enough, but something was missing. When he noticed Bekah brushing a llama someone had dropped off, he realized what his photo needed. "Hey, Bekah—got a sec?"

"Maybe," she replied in a suspicious tone. "What do you want?"

"A model." He'd meant to flatter her, but judging by the glare he was getting now, he'd missed the mark entirely. "I mean, someone to pose with the fawn. She's adorable, but I think it'd be an even nicer shot if we showed one of the people who've been taking care of her."

"Sierra's the one you should use, or one of the volunteers who have been here so long. They do all the hard stuff."

"But they're not as pretty as you."

"Will you stop?" Despite her protest, she laughed, which was what he'd been after in the first place. "I'm no prettier than anyone else who works here."

He disagreed wholeheartedly. A steady diet of his mother's cooking and a string of good nights' sleep had done wonders for the raggedy waif who'd blundered into town with a broken-down car and a nasty case of cynicism. She still wasn't the most outgoing person he'd ever come across, but she no longer ducked her head when she met new people coming into the center. Not to mention, she'd proven to be a quick study at everything she attempted.

Even Sierra was impressed, he mused with a grin. And she was notoriously hard to please.

Since he didn't want to push Bekah into accept-

ing his compliment—however sincere it might be—
he deftly switched tracks. "So, will you help me, or is
this little deer-y on her own?"

"I don't know what the other girls in town tell you,
but you are *so* not funny." Rolling her eyes at his play
on words, she finished with the llama and walked over
to join him. "What do you want me to do?"

"Just play with her like you do when you feed her
in the mornings. It's really cute, and I think we'll get
some good shots out of it."

"Okay."

She wound her ponytail around the top of her head
and picked up her discarded ball cap from a nearby
bale of hay. When she pulled it down low, it shaded
her face so he couldn't have recognized her in a sin-
gle-person lineup. Confused by the costume change,
he frowned. "What're you doing?"

"I don't mind being in the background, but I don't
want my face splashed all over the internet for people to see."

People, meaning Richie, Drew added silently. He
wished there was some way for him to assure Bekah
that she was finally safe from her abusive ex, but he'd
been around long enough to understand she had to
come to that realization on her own. "All right, we'll
do it your way."

She rewarded him with a bright smile, and he decided that giving in to her just this once hadn't been
so bad, after all.

Catching the small deer around the shoulders,
Bekah took an apple slice from the pocket of her coveralls and held it in her palm for the critter to sniff. Once
he'd gotten some stills, Drew discreetly toggled his

digital camera into video mode to catch the sight and sound of a true animal lover doing what she did best.

"Who's a good girl?" Bekah cooed, scratching the fawn up and down her back in a motion that made the animal squirm with delight. When the attention stopped for a few seconds, the deer butted against her in an unmistakable demand for more. Laughing, Bekah obliged her, and Drew kept the camera as steady as he could while he held in his own laughter.

There was nothing quite like watching her with the animals, he thought in honest admiration. It didn't take a genius to guess that she felt a connection with these lost and abandoned creatures, and they seemed to sense her compassion for them. She loved them, and they knew it.

When the small doe had gotten bored, Bekah let her go and brushed fur from the front of her pants. Then, out of nowhere, one of the pygmy goats hopped from the bale of straw he'd been standing on and into the pen with Bekah. Taking aim, he ran straight at her and bumped her hard enough to knock her back a step.

Drew kept the camera on them, capturing the spontaneous play session complete with the goat's nah-ing and Bekah's breathless laughter. He chased her around the pen, getting in a shot whenever he could, while the wide-eyed fawn watched their antics from a safe corner behind the water trough.

"I surrender!" Bekah finally announced, plopping down on the ground to make it official. The small goat danced and jumped in place, as if he was celebrating his victory over her. Being from a large extended family, Drew had seen his share of entertaining children, but he couldn't recall ever seeing anything quite so adorable.

"He's a real handful, isn't he?" Drew asked, capping his camera to protect the lens while he scratched the little terror between the ears.

"We found a family who wants to adopt him," Bekah told him with a bright smile. "They have a Great Dane who needs company when they're at work and school, and they thought this little guy would be perfect. They have a big, fenced yard, and three boys to play with. He should be really happy there."

Although she sounded pleased with the arrangement, Drew caught the wistful tinge in her voice. Stepping over the fence, he sat down on the edge of the water trough and gave her a sympathetic look. "You're gonna miss him, aren't you?"

"Yeah." Reaching out, she gathered him into her lap for a hug. "I'm gonna miss all of them when they go. But that's what we're supposed to do—find them a home or get them back to the wild where they belong. They aren't meant to stay here forever."

Something told him she wasn't only talking about the animals, and he felt his own mood sinking to match her tone. "Are you thinking the same thing about yourself?"

"I wish I could afford to stay," she confided sadly. "But much as I love it here, I have to be practical."

"If money's a problem—"

"It's the biggest one we have, which is why I'm working so hard on Animal Palooza. If we can make it through the year, the center has to have a full-time veterinarian," she argued in a maddeningly logical tone. "That's what the animals need more than any-thing, so that's where the money should go."

"But the staff—"

"Can be found anywhere," she said, cutting him off gently. "With a dedicated vet and Sierra, the hard stuff will be done by experts, and the general animal care can be handled by volunteers. I appreciate you trying to create a spot for me, Drew, but I've run the num-bers a hundred different ways, and that's the only way they work. Even then, it's a pretty thin line between this place staying open and closing."

"That's what the fund-raiser's all about," he re-minded her.

"Any extra money should go into a reserve fund, for repairs and other big expenses that crop up when you least expect them to. You can only patch the roof on the main building so many times before it has to be replaced."

"That's true enough, but you're great with the ani-mals. When Sierra gets to the end of the semester and is spending most of her time studying, you'll pretty much be running the place. These guys—" he mo-tioned around the pens filled with youngsters "—can't wait until finals are over."

Bekah processed that in silence, looking around her with a pensive expression. When her gaze came back to him, that stony resolve he'd seen before had mel-lowed considerably. "I hadn't thought of that. I have to stay until Sierra's tough classes are finished, anyway, or at least until she figures out I'm the worst tutor in history and fires me."

"She told me you're a fantastic tutor, and she doesn't

know how she'd ever have gotten through her midterms without you."

"That's ridiculous," Bekah scoffed, but the satisfied gleam in her eyes said otherwise. "She's a smart girl, and she would've figured out a way to pass those exams all on her own."

"Passing isn't enough for her," Drew commented with a chuckle. "She wants to blow the curve for everyone else."

"I've noticed she can be awfully competitive."

"Comes from being the middle child," he explained. "You're always trying to outdo one of your siblings. When I was younger, I was pretty much the same way."

Apparently he'd struck a chord with her, and she turned to him with curiosity sparkling in those soft blue eyes. "It's hard to believe that, since you're so easygoing now. What changed?"

"Our father died," he said quietly. "After that, our stupid rivalries didn't seem to matter anymore."

He didn't normally share that kind of detail about himself with anyone, not even his closest friends. He was Drew the Goof, the guy you could depend on for a good laugh when you needed one. His heart didn't often get dragged down by anything, but when it did, he felt compelled to mask his emotions with a smile.

Because that was who everyone expected him to be. The problem was, as he'd gotten older and life had become more serious, folks expected him to be the way he'd always been. And quite honestly, he'd outgrown the role of class clown years ago.

Bekah, on the other hand, didn't have those expectations. Because she'd met him so recently, her impression of him was still forming, which meant he had a chance to show her who he truly was beneath the smile he usually wore. But only if they spent enough time together for her to learn what he was really about.

He wasn't sure why her staying mattered so much to him. But it did, and he figured that if he waited long enough, it would eventually make sense.

"Drew, I'm sorry," she murmured, reaching out to cover his hand with her own. "I didn't mean to bring up sad times for you."

It was the first time she'd intentionally made physical contact with him, and he relished the feel of her soft skin on his. Forcing himself not to stare at their hands, he gave her a lopsided grin. "It's not all bad. I have great memories of him—we all do."

"When you keep someone in your heart, they're never really gone. My aunt Mary used to say that, and I always felt it was a nice thought."

"It is. Especially since it's true."

Bekah gave a delicate shrug, but she didn't pull her hand away. She seemed to be in a sharing mood, and he took the opportunity to learn a little more about what made this complicated woman tick. "You don't agree?"

"Maybe. Before I got here, most of the people I met weren't worth holding on to."

"What about now?"

That got him a shy smile. "There's a few I wouldn't mind keeping around."

"Am I one of 'em?"

"Maybe."

This smile had a hint of flirtatiousness in it, and he knew she'd intentionally repeated herself, adding the smirk for his benefit. Drew wasn't quite sure what was going on between them, but he knew he'd never forget this sunny afternoon he'd spent with Bekah and the animals.

The day when an edgy, closed-off runaway finally opened herself up to him and allowed him a glimpse of just how beautiful she was. Inside and out.

. It was the middle of the night when Bekah drifted out of a strange dream about a forest fire, disoriented by something she couldn't quite identify. While her brain gradually came into focus, she caught the sounds of bleating and whining coming from the baby barn. It must be a leftover image from her conversation with Sierra about caring for the wild infants, she reasoned as she rolled over to go back to sleep.

Then she smelled smoke.

Bolting upright in bed, she snapped on the lights, squinting against the sudden brightness while she stumbled around searching for her barn boots. She found them under the small kitchen table where she'd left them and pulled them on over her bare feet.

She nearly yanked the door off its hinges in her haste to get moving. Running for all she was worth, she paused outside the window in the side door of the stock barn and braced herself for what she might see inside.

When she forced herself to look, to her immense relief there were no flames. A hazy curtain of smoke hung in the air, and the animals were clearly agitated, but other than that, they seemed fine. She raced around back and saw what had awakened her from a dead sleep.

The storage barn was on fire.

Fueled by stacks of hay and straw, not to mention dozens of bales of dry wood shavings, flames were finding crevices in the weathered walls and climbing into the dark sky. While the animals weren't in immediate danger, if the fire couldn't be stopped, it wouldn't take long for it to reach the two wild-animal barns and, just beyond that, the kennels and animal hospital.

She let herself into the clinic and picked up the cordless phone from its charging stand. With trembling hands, Bekah dialed the one local number other than the center that she knew by heart. Thankfully, Drew answered on the first ring.

"Bekah, what's wrong?"

"The feed barn is on fire," she answered crisply. "We need hands here. Lots of them."

Leaving him to figure out the rest, she clicked the phone off and headed into the baby barn to start moving the helpless wild orphans someplace safer. The small ones would be easy enough, but the larger animals were another story. She might be able to coax the terrified creatures out of their pens, but then where would she put them?

Hoping an answer would come to her, she started with the cages. They were covered in dark canvas, which seemed to be keeping the birds inside them reasonably calm, so Bekah left the fabric on. She couldn't resist peeking inside Rosie's and found a pair of glittering black eyes staring back at her. The hawk didn't seem panicked, though, which Bekah took as a good sign.

"That's my brave girl," Bekah murmured, lifting the cage carefully to avoid jostling its occupant. "We'll get through this, won't we?"

Rosie squawked in reply, and Bekah couldn't help smiling at the thought that the hawk seemed to be trying to reassure her, too. Once she'd moved everything she could lift alone, she faced the pens holding an assortment of understandably nervous animals and waited for inspiration.

Nothing.

So, since there was no other choice, she waded into the goat enclosure and scooped up the tamest pygmy nanny they had. Clearly terrified, she struggled in Bekah's arms, bleating at the top of her lungs the whole way out to the temporary corral they kept out front for visiting days. There was a roof over top of it, so they'd be dry and out of the way of the rescue team here. Stopping to catch her breath, she felt her spirits dropping. If they all fought her like this, how on earth would she get them out safely?

Her answer came in the glare of headlights, and she turned to see a heavy-duty pickup hauling a long stock trailer imprinted with the Gallimore Stables logo. It circled the side yard and neatly backed up near the door she was using to evacuate the animals.

When Drew stepped out of the cab, without thinking she launched herself at him in a grateful hug. When she realized what she'd done, she got a grip on her runaway emotions and shook her head. "Sorry."

"No problem. Everyone else is on their way over. What can we do?"

It was then that she realized his two brothers were climbing down from the truck cab, and she felt her cheeks warming with embarrassment. "I'm trying to move the babies, but they're all panicked, and some of them won't cooperate. I'm not strong enough to lift them on my own."

Mike and Josh headed inside, their hands filled with what looked like dark hoods.

"What are they carrying?" she asked.

"When we've got a horse that won't go into the trailer, we cover its eyes, and it doesn't give us so much trouble. We're hoping it'll work with these guys, too," he explained while he lowered the trailer's large rear door to form a ramp.

Clearly, they'd handled frightened animals before, she thought with relief as she hurried inside the compartment to follow his instructions. By the time Mike and Josh emerged with two blindfolded fawns, Drew and Bekah were inside the trailer waiting to man the movable partitions that would separate the various species from each other.

"Fire department's on their way," Mike told them as they passed each other. "I told them not to use the siren, but—"

A loud wail sounded in the distance, and Bekah fought the urge to scream in frustration. "These animals are scared enough already. That's only going to make it harder for us to handle them."

"I'm on it," Drew assured her, clicking his phone on. After a moment, he said, "Sierra, it's me. Where are you?" When he had an answer, he went on, "You need to connect with the fire trucks headed this way and tell them to shut off their sirens before they scare every critter here to death."

Apparently, he got the response he was after, because he hung up without saying anything more and got back to work. They were making good progress in clearing out the baby barn when two older fire trucks roared into the parking lot and skidded to a halt in the loose gravel. Josh motioned toward the source of the blaze, and they continued on to the storage building that was now fully engulfed in flames.

While the crew fought to bring the fire under some semblance of control, Mike and Josh made several trips down the lane to the horse farm to get the wild animals settled in an empty barn. Meanwhile, Drew and Bekah dragged, carried and hauled tamer tenants from the kennels and lined up their cages under the picnic pavilion out front to wait for their turn in the trailer.

"Don't worry, Bekah," Drew's younger sister, Erin, told her confidently. "They're scared, but no one's hurt. I'll keep an eye on them while you're relocating the others."

That was when she realized that at some point, most of the Kinley clan had gathered at the center. She was glad to see Maggie, Lily and the kids weren't there, because this was no place for children. Plenty of people she'd never met were lending a hand, and two of the firefighters were juggling a family of ducks that was making a concerted attempt to escape the chaotic scene.

Seeing all these people working together to save the animals was so touching, it caught her completely by surprise.

Uncharacteristic tears flooded her eyes, and she blinked them away while she swallowed down the lump that had suddenly formed in her throat. Hard as she was trying to keep it together, she knew she wasn't doing a very good job when Drew appeared beside her, concern clouding his eyes.

"You okay?"

Not trusting herself to speak without sobbing, she

nodded and took a deep breath to steady her voice. "It's just so remarkable how everyone came to help in the middle of the night like this."

"We've done the same for them over the years," he explained in a gentle tone. "That's what neighbors do."

"I've never had that, I guess," she confided, whisking away a few tears that had broken free of her control. Gazing up at this man who'd come to her rescue time and again, she said, "It's nice to know you're not all alone, isn't it?"

"Yeah, it is."

Gathering her into his arms, he deftly turned her away from the smoky view. His well-worn T-shirt felt soft against her skin, and beneath her cheek she felt the steady, comforting beat of a heart that had proven to be much larger than she ever could have imagined.

After indulging in a few moments of relative quiet, she pulled herself together and got practical. "I think I've done all I can here. I should get over to the farm and make sure our critters are all okay."

"You got it." Motioning her ahead of him, he walked her over to the truck he'd driven in, which was loaded down with the last of the cages ready for transport. Once they were on their way, he said, "Your place probably isn't livable right now. Would you like to stay at the farm until we fumigate your stuff?"

"Definitely," she agreed with a yawn. Looking over her shoulder to check on their passengers, she went on, "Do you have a cot and sleeping bag I can borrow?"

"Sure. Why?"

"These poor guys have been through a lot, and I'm sure they're still terrified. I want to stay in the barn with them to help them settle in better."

"That's real thoughtful of you, but you need a better night's sleep than you'll get out there. I'm sure they'll be fine."

Sometimes this intelligent man could be incredibly dense. "Did you ever have a sick pet?"

"A few times."

"What did you do?"

"Okay, you got me," Drew admitted with a chuckle. "I snuck 'em upstairs and let 'em sleep on my bed."

"Well, I can't do that with this many, so I'll have to settle for the opposite. Your barns are clean enough for most people to live in. Trust me—I've slept in worse places."

He didn't say anything to that, telling her she'd made her point. When they came around the last turn in the lane, she was stunned to find the big farmhouse and front two barns fully lit up. She got the impression that they were drawing the frightened animals toward a safe, comfortable place to spend the night, like beacons in the darkness.

And her, too, she realized with exhausted gratitude. Because she knew how it felt to be lost and terrified about what might happen to her. Now that she'd found another way to live, she was happy to have those dark days behind her.

Drew backed toward the open barn doors, and they climbed out to start arranging cages inside the cleared-out storage space Erin had reserved for their whimpering cargo. After one trip, Drew paused to stare at nothing in particular.

"Hey, Bekah," he began in the tone that alerted her he was making things up as he went along. "What if we put a laptop up on that shelf over there? We could use a webcam to keep tabs on these guys so you could sleep in the house. Can you make it transmit without sending the signal out to the internet?"

After considering his suggestion for a moment, she asked, "You mean, like a closed-circuit video?"

"I don't know," he replied with a grin. "That brainy stuff is your department."

Not long ago, she would have assumed that he was handing her a line and not have taken it very well. But now, despite the awful night she'd been having, she couldn't help smiling at the compliment. "You're not so bad yourself."

"Thanks. Whattya think of my idea?"

Stepping closer, she stood on tiptoe to kiss his cheek. "I think it's brilliant."

"Just don't tell anyone I came up with it, okay? They'll start expecting me to be a genius all the time."

"Your secret's safe with me."

Chapter Six

Sunday morning, Drew pulled in at the clinic on his way to the farm. Getting out of his truck, he surveyed the grim scene with a frown. The feed barn was still standing, but that was about the only positive thing he could say about it. The firefighters had peeled back enormous sections of the metal roofing to access the interior and douse the flames from above, and the gaping holes in the walls had left them barely capable of supporting what was left of the structure.

A thin haze of smoke still hung in the air, and while the fire had been contained to the single barn, the walls and windows of the other buildings were smeared with black soot marks. Since it was closest to the storage space, the baby barn had taken the brunt of the heat and smoke, and he grimaced when he noted just how close the fire had come to the helpless animals inside.

Quite honestly, Drew thought morosely, the formerly peaceful clearing in the woods looked like a disaster zone. He couldn't begin to calculate how long it would take them to get everything back to normal.

It wasn't like him to be so negative, and he gladly

headed down the well-used lane in search of some-thing to lift his spirits. He found it in the stable near-est the house, and he gratefully walked toward the joyful sound.

"Aren't you good boys?" Bekah's voice reached him through the open sliding door, her laughter drawing him in a step at a time. "If you keep eating like this, you'll be the biggest ones of the bunch."

Drew paused outside the makeshift holding area, watching her bottle-feed two goats at once. She made it look easy, and he could hardly believe she hadn't been doing this kind of job for years.

When she noticed him, her eyes lit up with un-abashed delight. "There's my hero. How are you doing?"

"Well enough, considering." Glancing around, he registered the fact that all the morning chores she nor-mally handled had already been done. "Did you ever go to sleep?"

"I crashed for a couple hours on the living room sofa after everyone left, but the animals are used to getting breakfast at seven, and I could hear them on the web-cam. They're better than an alarm clock."

"No doubt." Pleased to find that her harrowing ad-venture hadn't done anything to dampen her spirits, he shook off his own dark mood and got practical. "What can I do to help?"

"Nothing for now. Later, there will be plenty to do inside the clinic."

"Lotta smoke damage, huh?"

She groaned. "It's everywhere. It's going to take forever for us to scrub everything down well enough for the animals to go back in."

No mention of her own living space, he noted with

admiration. Most folks he knew would've complained about the fact that their apartment was in the same kind of shape as the other buildings. Bekah's difficult background made her selfless streak all the more impressive.

Drew squinted up and saw nothing but blue sky. "Fortunately, it's supposed to be a gorgeous day, so we should be able to get a lot done."

"Us and what army?"

"Never underestimate a Kinley," he cautioned her. "I'll come over to help after church and show you how much we can get done in an afternoon."

His mention of Sunday services seemed to interest her, and her curious look quickly gave way to a thoughtful one. "Drew?"

"Yeah?"

She hesitated, as if she was running what she wanted to tell him through her head before saying it out loud. Someday, he hoped she'd trust him enough to just spit things out rather than cautiously editing her comments ahead of time. "Do you think God brought me here that day when I got lost on my way to that interview?"

"Definitely," he replied, stunned to hear her voicing an idea that had occurred to him more than once.

"Well, if He did, why do you think He'd do something like that?"

To save me from myself.

The response came into his mind fully formed, so clear to him that he knew it was the truth. Unfortunately, he had a hunch that kind of answer would send Bekah back into her shell—or worse, running away from him in a panic. Now that she seemed comfortable in his hometown, the last thing he wanted to do was spook her into leaving. He was very tempted to come back with the usual "God works in mysterious ways," but Drew suspected she wouldn't take that very well. Bekah was a sharp lady, and she'd recognize a dodge when she heard one.

So he let his mind wander around until it came up with a vague but reasonable explanation. "He knew you were needed here in Oaks Crossing, so that's where He sent you."

"But how did He know the clinic needed my help?"

Having grown up with the faith his parents had always valued above everything else, Drew didn't know how to respond. To his mind, you either believed in God or you didn't. But his instincts were telling him that Bekah needed better guidance than that, and after mulling it over, he came up with a way for her to discover the truth for herself.

"You could come to church with the family and me," he suggested. "Maybe you'll find the answer you're looking for there."

By framing it as a family outing, he was hoping to remove any sensitive personal issues from the equation. He still wasn't certain what was going on between them, but he didn't want her opinion of him—good or bad—to sway her decision. He firmly believed that having a connection with God would do her no end of good, but he recognized that he couldn't create that bond for her. If she decided it was something she wanted, she'd have to forge it on her own.

"I don't know," she hedged, the anxious tone he despised creeping back into her voice. "I haven't been to a church service since I was a kid."

"No one else is gonna know that."

"I do," she argued. "God does."

Her sense of right and wrong was so deeply ingrained in her character, he knew it had somehow been wired into her at birth. From what he'd learned about her background, he was amazed that she'd managed to hold on to her integrity through it all. There must have been times when that was all she had. Now that she seemed more comfortable in Oaks Crossing, he prayed those dark days were behind her and she wouldn't have to struggle so hard to make her way.

"True enough, but I don't think He blames kids for mistakes their parents make. To Him, the important thing is what you do from here on out."

She chewed on that for a few seconds, then turned to him with a wry grin. "I don't sing very well."

"Neither do I," he assured her with a laugh. "We'll make a great pair."

Taking a deep breath, she finally relented. "Okay, I'll try it. Will you sit with me?"

"Absolutely. I'd never leave a pretty lady sitting all alone."

"Yeah," she retorted with a very feminine smirk. "I've heard that about you."

"You really have to quit talking to Sierra," he objected with a mock growl. "She doesn't know half as much about me as she thinks she does."

"Really? What doesn't she know?"

"She has no clue I like photography," he pointed out almost immediately. "No one does except for you."

"Why not?"

"It's my thing, and I like keeping it to myself."

"But you shared it with me," Bekah reminded him with a curious expression. "What's so special about me?"

Pretty much everything, he answered silently. He'd never met a woman with her blend of looks and intelligence, not to mention the depth of compassion she showed to animals and the few people she felt she could trust. "You've got a lot going for you, whether you realize it or not."

"Thanks. That's sweet of you to say."

She angled her head away from him, making it clear that she'd interpreted his sincere comment as some kind of line. Since he didn't know how to remedy the situation without making her uncomfortable, he decided it was best to let the subject drop.

But someday, when he told her something like that, she'd believe him. He'd just have to keep trying until it finally happened.

In the meantime, he settled for sliding a bottle from the milk carrier. "I'll take over out here so you can get ready for church. You and Lily are about the same size, and I'm sure she'll loan you something to wear."

"I'd really like to go," she argued faintly, "but I've got way too much to do."

"They're all fine, and the work will still be here in a couple hours. A lot of the folks who came last night to help will be at the service, and you'll get a chance to meet them under nicer circumstances."

"It would be great if I could tell them how much I appreciated them being there," she said in a brighter tone.

"Then go get ready. I can handle these guys."

"Well…okay." After filling him in on which of

the critters still needed to be fed, she hurried into the house.

Moving around the stalls, he added fresh water to the troughs, then filled each food bowl from the stock of provisions she'd efficiently lined up along the walls. When he was finished with them, he went to the large birdcages sitting in the tack room that had been cleared of saddles to make room for them. The eagle cracked open a disinterested eye before returning to his dozing, and a large hoot owl studied him as if trying to determine whether or not he'd make a decent meal.

Untamed as the forest that surrounded the farm, the wild birds touched a part of Drew that nothing else ever had. As a child, he'd often admired them from the ground, while they circled lazily overhead hunting for their next meal. Even now that he was older, he couldn't help envying them their freedom.

He'd spent his entire life on these few hundred acres of an infinitely larger world. How would it be, he'd often wondered, to be able to take off and go whenever you wanted, zooming away to pursue whatever caught your eye? Then, as it so often did lately, his mind drifted to Colorado, and whether it was a foolish venture or the opportunity of a lifetime. One minute, he leaned toward the first, and in the next he was convinced it was the right move for him.

What about his family? he asked himself for the countless time. Things had been precarious enough for the farm and the center before the fire, but now they were even worse. Insurance would cover replacing the barn itself, but the contents were another story. Putting in an extra round of hay would help, but Mike and Josh would need help getting it planted and harvested. How could he possibly turn his back on all that and fly off into the sunset as if nothing had happened?

A familiar squawk nudged him from his brooding, and he approached Rosie's cage with a chuckle. "I didn't forget you, girl. Hang on a sec."

Fortunately, today was a mellow food day for the predators, so he doled out chicken for each of them and replaced their water. While they ate, he deftly slid the cage bottoms out and cleaned them without disturbing the birds.

By the time he was finished with his animal-care circuit, Bekah rejoined him, freshly scrubbed and wearing something he'd never seen on her.

"That's pretty," he complimented her, admiring the floral-print dress with a smile. "Just your style."

"It's Erin's. Or was, anyway. When I asked if I could borrow something to wear for church, your mom found this upstairs in her old closet and told me to keep it. I'm pretty sure she pulled a price tag off the sleeve before she handed it to me."

"Yeah, Erin's never been keen about getting dressed up." When he noticed Bekah trying to discreetly check his handiwork, he smothered a grin. "So, how'd I do?"

"Everyone looks happy." Gazing up at him, she gave him a grateful smile. "Thanks, Drew."

Returning the smile, it occurred to him that he couldn't really think of anything he wouldn't do to see her look at him like he was Superman. "It was no problem. I'll just wash up and we'll get going."

"Take your time," she told him, sitting down at one of the picnic tables and glancing around her with another smile. "It's a beautiful morning."

It sure was, he thought as he headed inside. One of

the prettiest he'd ever seen. When he was ready, he met her out front and walked her to his truck. Once they were in the cab, he started the engine and headed for town. "Forgot to mention I found a mechanic who's willing to work on your car at the center so we don't have to tow it anywhere. He's coming out Thursday afternoon."

"I don't have the money to pay him yet," she informed him curtly. "You should've asked me first."

He put her uncharacteristic irritability down to fatigue and summoned patience into his tone. "Guys like that aren't easy to find, especially since he's gotta do all the diagnostic work the old-fashioned way. I had to grab him while he had the time to do it."

"I get that, but I still don't have the money."

"Well…"

"Please, don't tell me you paid him up front."

Glancing over, he added what he hoped was an apologetic grin. "I'm your hero. Remember?"

Crickets.

He could almost feel her glowering at him, and he reminded himself that she'd been burned in her last relationship because she'd believed in the wrong guy. It was understandable that she'd want to take care of things herself to avoid having to deal with any more problems. Trust was a huge issue for her, and he was smart enough to recognize that there weren't sufficient words in his vocabulary to convince her he was trustworthy.

He just had to keep proving it to her, day by day, gesture by gesture, until she eventually believed that he had her best interests at heart. Until then, he'd have to be patient and hang in there with her.

"Since you're already mad at me, here." Fishing a cell phone out of his shirt pocket, he handed it over.

She hit the power button and let out an exasperated sigh. "This is brand-new. What on earth were you thinking?"

"It's one of those prepaid phones, and I promise it's the cheapest one I could find." She glared at him, and he took that as his cue to continue. He could be changing her mind or digging his own grave. Either way, he was determined to make sure she understood why he'd gone behind her back that way. "I don't want you out here by yourself with a dud of a car and no way to call for help. If you hadn't been able to get into the clinic last night for some reason, that fire could've ended up being a catastrophe. All I did was charge the phone and put some minutes on it for you. After that, you can either buy more time for it or chuck it in the trash. Totally up to you."

When she didn't respond, he suspected that anything else he might say would only get hurled back in his face. So he kept his mouth shut and drove the rest of the way to town in silence.

When he turned onto Main Street, she finally broke down and said, "Thank you."

"Anytime."

Swiveling to face him squarely, she asked, "You really mean that, don't you?"

"Yup."

"Most guys talk a good game but end up dropping the ball when it really counts."

"A sports metaphor?" he teased with a grin. "Very impressive. Speaking of which, I noticed the Bears are playing tonight. Wanna come watch it with us at the farm?"

"That depends. Will you guys all be rooting for Cincinnati?"

"Got that right. But since you're a loyal fan of the opposition, we won't give you a hard time. Much."

"Then I'll be there."

Everything had to be qualified and analyzed before she made a commitment, Drew noted darkly. He wondered if she'd ever feel safe enough to do something on a whim. Then again, he thought as he pulled into the church parking lot, this morning she was attending her first religious service in years. Maybe this would mark the start of better things to come.

When he rounded the truck to open the passenger door for her, she didn't move. Staring at the small white chapel, she met his eyes with a hesitant look. "Is your family here?"

Scanning the lot, he found their cars and nodded. "I didn't tell 'em you were coming, though, in case you changed your mind."

"I almost did," she confided softly. "And it wasn't because I had too much to do."

"New things are scary," he reasoned as calmly as he could. "But it's good to try them anyway. You never know what you might find when you're not looking."

Tilting her head, she gave him a thoughtful look. "Did you make that up?"

"Nah, that's one of my dad's. He had a way of making tough things sound less intimidating."

"Everyone talks about him so often, it's obvious you all love him very much. I wish I could've met him."

"I do, too," Drew said, adding a crooked grin. "He would've liked your spunk."

That got him a delighted little girl's smile. "You think I'm spunky?"

"Sure do. I'm guessing you don't see yourself that way."

She considered that for a moment and shrugged. "Before I came here, the face in my mirror mostly looked exhausted, terrified or a depressing combination of the two."

He picked up on her reference to the past and seized on the thread of hope he heard in her voice. "And now?"

"Still tired." A shy smile tugged at the corner of her mouth. "But not so terrified anymore."

The confession was so personal, he felt as if she'd just shared her biggest secret with him. Knowing she trusted him with such an intimate detail about herself made his chest swell with pride, and he didn't bother hiding his delight. "That's great, Bekah. You've come a long way."

"But I still have so far to go," she informed him with a sigh. Her eyes flicked to the church again, then came back to him. "Do you think God will be happy to see me?"

"Definitely. He likes girls with spunk, too."

A quick laugh chased the worry from her delicate features, and he offered her his hand to step down to the pavement. As they made their way up the steps and into the entryway, he stayed close but was careful to give her some space. She'd made it plain that she wanted to make her own way from now on, and the last thing he wanted to do was cause her to feel crowded.

Some of the people milling around the sanctuary had met her during their visits to the rescue center, and they all greeted her as if she'd been attending services with them for years. Since she couldn't see him behind her, Drew nodded to each person in turn, silently thanking them for going out of their way to make this lost sheep feel welcome.

"Hi, Uncle Drew!" Abby hung over the back of the Kinleys' customary pew, excitedly waving to them as if she hadn't seen them in months. When they stopped at the end of the row, she added, "Mommy told me about the fire. How are all the animals doing?"

"Just fine, thanks to everyone who came to help out."

"That's good. Parker and me thought you'd be tired, so we saved seats for you."

Beside her, the foster child she called her cousin looked up from his bulletin with a faint smile so fleeting, Drew almost missed it. Undeterred, he reached over and ruffled the boy's light brown mop of hair. "How's it goin', dude?"

"Okay," he murmured, glancing up at Erin.

She gave him an overly bright smile and nudged his shoulder. "You should tell Drew about your science award."

"You build a rocket in that shed out back of your house?" Drew asked, hoping to coax a smile from him. To say the kid had been through a lot was an understatement, and the whole family was determined to do whatever they could for him.

"I can't build a rocket," Parker informed him with a slightly more confident grin. "I'm just a kid."

Bingo, Drew thought with a mental fist pump. Pulling a serious face, he pretended to mull that over. "I don't know. Kids are pretty smart these days, with computers and all. I mean, your phone does more than the first laptop I had."

"Really?" he asked, clearly stunned that Drew had managed to survive. "That's weird."

"Tell me about it," Drew muttered, taking his seat beside Bekah as the organist started the first hymn.

"I just want to remind you," she whispered while he opened the hymnal to the right page, "I'm a terrible singer. If you want me to sit in the back where you can't hear me, I won't be offended."

"Back at ya."

They traded quiet chuckles and then did their best to hit some of the same notes the choir was singing. When Bekah smiled up at him midverse, Drew felt his heart roll over in his chest like one of the shelter puppies who did cute tricks to get her attention. Startled by the unfamiliar sensation, he tried to remember another time when a woman had caused that kind of reaction in him.

Hard as he tried, he came up blank. Even Kelly, much as he'd loved her, hadn't reached this deeply into the heart of who he was. That Bekah had a unique effect on him meant something, he was certain. Something important that neither of them was ready for. The trouble was, he didn't know how to stop feeling whatever it was he was feeling. He'd better figure it out fast, though, so he could come up with a way to put an end to it.

Because with his own plans so up in the air, this was no time to get attached.

In all her travels, Bekah had never felt more at peace anywhere than she did in this quaint country chapel.

Although the morning was chilly, the clear sky was a brilliant blue without a hint of clouds to mar it. She wasn't sure if it was the weather or the fact that she was sitting with Drew, but it was almost as if the day's sunny optimism was contagious, and she'd caught it in spite of the exhaustion her long, harrowing night had left behind.

Then again, she thought while the choir finished singing a pleasant hymn, maybe it had something to do with the fact that for the first time since her childhood, she was in church. Her earlier nervousness had evaporated in the face of the congregation's welcoming attitude toward her. Right after asking about her, most of them had inquired about how the animals had come through their middle-of-the-night ordeal.

In truth, their concern for the center's residents hadn't surprised her all that much. People around the area were familiar with the clinic and the good work it was doing, so it wasn't unusual for them to show an interest in what was going on there. But their questions about her own well-being touched her very much. Since she'd been on her own for so long, she'd grown accustomed to drifting in and out of people's lives without leaving much of a mark.

Apparently, she mused with a little smile, Oaks Crossing was an entirely different sort of place. While she wouldn't be able to quietly slide out of town when her instincts told her it was time to go, she was starting to believe that forfeiting her usual anonymity for a sense of community—even for a little while—would be a worthwhile trade.

When Pastor Wheaton stepped up to the podium to begin his sermon, she dragged her mind back from its wandering, reminding herself that it was rude to day-dream when a preacher was speaking. Fortunately for her, once he started talking, the modest-looking man in the gray suit had her complete attention.

"Good morning," he said, winging a fatherly smile around the congregation. Once they'd responded, he picked up a set of notes and frowned down at the pages in his hand. Showing a remarkable flair for the dramatic, he flung them over his shoulder and rested his arms across the lectern, hands folded while he gazed out into the hushed crowd.

With a very un-pastorly grin, he confided, "Not really what I wanted to say this morning. In light of recent events, I think something else would be better. As many of you know, the Oaks Crossing Rescue Center suffered a fire earlier today. No animals or people were harmed, and I want to thank our volunteer firefighters and everyone else who drove over to help the Kinleys keep the damage to a minimum. My wife and I will be heading out there after lunch to assist in the cleanup. The more hands, the lighter the work, so if you can spare an hour or two, I hope you'll join us."

He went on to mention the fine work the staff members were doing and how their ongoing efforts were making the world a better place for so many of God's creatures. His gaze roamed over the crowd, but at one point, Bekah felt it land squarely on her. "Often, when we feel lost, we wonder if anyone knows. Or cares."

There was a general ripple of movement and murmured comments, and Bekah realized she wasn't the only one who felt as if the pastor was speaking to her directly. With an understanding smile, he continued, "Our Heavenly Father does see us when we struggle, but sometimes He chooses to let us find our own way out. Hard as it is, loving parents have to do that sometimes so their children will learn the lessons they need to have a good life."

Bekah's heart was pounding so loud, she was convinced that everyone around her must have been able to hear it. In those simple, straightforward words, she found the answer she'd been searching for since leaving her parents' home after finishing high school. Crazy as it seemed, in her heart she knew this was the explanation for why she'd landed in Oaks Crossing. It didn't escape her that Drew had been the one to suggest it, long before Pastor Wheaton decided to put aside his planned sermon to teach Bekah something that she didn't even realize she needed to know.

It was all about love, she realized with a smile. While she hadn't experienced much of it recently, here she was surrounded by it every day, from people who honestly cared about others and what was happening in their lives. And it wasn't just the Kinley family, she'd noticed. Whether things were going well or badly, the residents of this small Kentucky town lifted each other up, confident that if a time came when they needed the same, their neighbors would be there for them.

For someone who'd been crawling along weighed down by a bruised spirit, that approach to life was beyond generous. It was a blessing.

When the service was over, everyone stood but

didn't rush to the doors the way she'd expected. Instead, they lingered near their seats and in the aisles, taking a few minutes to chat with their friends. She heard snippets of a few different conversations about today's football game and saw phones and photos of grandkids being passed around. There was plenty of laughter, and while they must all have other things to do, no one seemed in a hurry to leave.

Then, to her surprise, someone tapped her on the shoulder. When she turned, a white-haired woman with rosy cheeks beamed at her. "You don't know me, but I adopted my Bessie from the rescue center last year. She's the sweetest little dog in the world, and I can't tell you how much she means to me."

"I—"

"Those animals might have all died if you hadn't been there last night to save them," the woman continued. "God bless you."

Totally at a loss for how to respond, Bekah sent a help-me look up at Drew, who smoothly stepped in. "Our Bekah's something else, that's for sure."

Our Bekah. She liked the way that sounded, and the fondness twinkling in his eyes bolstered her confidence enough for her to thank the woman.

"You're very welcome, dear. I'm going home now to start cooking."

Bekah was confused about why she'd share that detail but asked, "That sounds nice. What are you making?"

"Vera's specialty is fried chicken," Drew informed her with a grin of anticipation. "Be sure to make a little extra for me," he added with a wink.

The woman clucked her tongue but smiled at Bekah.

"Drew and his leftovers. If it weren't for Maggie and her friends, I think this poor boy would starve."

He chuckled. "It's a good thing for me that there're so many great chefs in town. Like Bekah, for instance. Just ask the family—she makes a mean Western omelet."

Vera's eyes lit with interest, and she said, "Well, I should be going. I'll see you at the center later on."

Once she was gone, Bekah turned to Drew, more than a little aggravated. "What were you thinking, mentioning that we had breakfast together? Now she's going to tell everyone we're seeing each other."

"Trust me, darlin'," he assured her as he nudged her out into the aisle, "as efficient as the Oaks Crossing gossip mill is, they already think we are."

"But you just made it sound like it's the truth."

"Is that a problem?"

Was it? she wondered as they followed the line of people going down the steps. The answer should have been easy: yes or no. But Bekah found herself in the unfamiliar position of not knowing what she thought. Up to now, her life had been dominated by extremely simple decisions. Go or stay. Fix her car's radiator or pay her rent. Replace her threadbare coat or save the money for the inevitable rainy day.

But this time, the question made her pause and reflect on what she truly wanted. Living under Richie's thumb had made her value her independence above everything else. But spending so much of her time with Drew had shown her possibilities she hadn't even considered before meeting the outgoing man who'd thought nothing of taking in a complete stranger and making her feel safe.

At the bottom of the steps, he gently took her arm and guided her beneath a large oak that had shed most of its leaves into a crunchy pile on the grass. Gazing down at her, he frowned. "I assumed you wouldn't mind folks knowing we're friends. Was I wrong?"

For some reason, her heart drooped a bit, and she bit back a sigh. He thought they were just friends, and she couldn't blame him for that. She'd resolutely kept him at arm's length ever since they met, giving him no reason to think of her otherwise.

"No, it's fine," she finally said, searching for a way to justify her odd behavior. She was more than a little relieved when she hit on one she thought he'd accept. "I'm just not used to small-town gossip, I guess. Where I'm from, even next-door neighbors don't really know each other."

"I can't imagine that," he commented with a chuckle. "Around here, sometimes folks know what's going on with me before I do. And then they tell Mom."

"Awkward." Grinning, she couldn't help thinking it was kind of cute how this tall, capable man was still intimidated by his petite mother.

"Tell me about it. I've only proposed once, but according to the hens, she's had about a dozen prospective daughters-in-law."

The revelation absolutely floored her, and she didn't bother trying to hide her shock. "Who on earth would turn you down?"

He shrugged. "Someone who was looking for something different than I was."

Even though it was absolutely none of her business, she couldn't help asking, "And what are you looking for?"

"I'm not sure. I figure I'll know it when I see it."

Something she couldn't begin to define warmed the gold in his eyes, pulling her closer even though he hadn't moved. Completely mesmerized, she couldn't have looked away if she'd tried. Searching her paralyzed brain for words, she finally came up with "Okay."

The corner of his mouth quirked with a grin, and the moment passed by like a gust of wind that nearly knocks you over and then vanishes.

"We'd best get to the center," he said, stepping back for her to go ahead of him. "From what you said earlier, we've got a lotta work to do before we can move the animals back in."

His quick switch from intensely personal to all-business nearly gave her whiplash, and she had no idea how to respond. Unable to come up with anything better, she nodded and followed him to his truck.

All the way out to the farm, she couldn't shake the feeling that something very important had just happened between them. But because she'd never experienced it before, she couldn't quite put her finger on what it was.

Chapter Seven

After dropping Bekah at the clinic, Drew swung by the farm. When he walked into the kitchen, he let out a low whistle of appreciation. "Mom, you've outdone yourself. Again."

"Do you think it's enough food?" she asked, surveying the loaded-down table and counters with an anxious expression.

"For an army."

She beamed at him, then nudged him with an elbow. "Don't you worry. I made plenty of extra for you this week. There's a stack of plastic containers in the fridge on the back porch."

"Awesome. You know I'd die of hunger without you, right?"

"That's not what I heard from my friends after church this morning," she teased with a knowing smile. "Speaking of which, how's Bekah today?"

Drew wasn't quite sure how to answer that. He didn't want to get her hopes up about him finally finding someone to be serious about, but he couldn't deny that of all the women he'd dated, Bekah Holloway was by far the most intriguing of the bunch. Because he wasn't ready to share that with anyone, he kept it simple. "Fine."

"Fine," she mimicked, adding a long-suffering sigh. "I wish your father was here, God rest him. You'd tell him everything that's rattling around in that head of yours, and then he'd tell me, and I could quit wondering what in the world is going on with you."

"Whattya mean?" he asked, popping a grape into his mouth. "If there was anything to tell, I would. It's not like I live to torture you the way Mike does."

"Our darling Lily has softened a lot of that out of him," she said, affection bringing out the Irish lilt that still crept into her voice now and then. "I'm hoping someday you'll find the one to help you do the same."

"Well, when I do you'll be the first to know. I promise."

She rewarded him with a proud mother's smile. "That's my boy. You know you're my favorite, don't you?"

Drew grinned. It was an old family joke among the Kinleys, because all of them had been her favorite— and the bane of her existence—at one time or another. Standing, he kissed her cheek before picking up a huge camping jug full of ice water. "Yeah, I know. See you over there?"

"As soon as I make a few more peanut-butter-and-jelly sandwiches for the kids."

Nodding, he lugged the water out to his truck and lifted it into the bed before returning for more of the food and drinks Mom had been preparing. Once he had it all, he closed the tailgate to keep everything from sliding out onto the rough field road that led to the rescue center. When he drove over the small hill, he couldn't keep back a smile.

There were at least a dozen cars and trucks parked in the grass near the road, and some genius had thought to drop a Dumpster next to the ruined barn. Some of the same firefighters who'd answered the early-morning call were there, dressed in protective gear while they poked through the rubble, searching for hot spots. Behind them, volunteers armed with pitchforks had started dumping waterlogged hay and straw into wheelbarrows that other people wheeled up the Dumpster's ramp before heading back for more.

Because of the old barn wood and piles of pine shavings, the air smelled more like a campfire than a disaster. Thank God for small blessings, Drew thought as he angled his truck into a tight spot near the refreshment tables Lily, Abby and Parker were setting up.

"This is a nice spot," he said approvingly as he brought in his first load. "Who picked it out?"

"I did," Parker confided quietly. "I thought people would be cooler in the shade."

That was the longest sentence he'd ever heard the kid say, and Drew rewarded his courage with a broad grin. "Great idea. Where would you like the drinks?"

The boy glanced timidly at Lily, who smiled at him. "It's your call, Parker. You're in charge."

"Yeah?" Drew asked. "How'd you manage that?"

"We drew straws," Abby informed him proudly. "Parker's was the longest, so he gets to be the captain today."

Over their heads, Drew met Lily's eyes, and by the twinkle in them, he assumed the kindhearted teacher had devised a way to make sure Erin's shy foster son got a turn in the spotlight.

"Maybe you can talk your daddy into doing that at the farm," Drew said. "I wouldn't mind being in charge once in a while."

"You should tell him that," Abby suggested in her fearless way.

"You think he'd listen?"

"Sure. If he doesn't, you can tell Grammy. She'll take care of it."

"I'll keep that in mind, cowgirl," Drew agreed with a grin. "Thanks for the suggestion."

"You're welcome."

"Man," he muttered to Lily as she followed him to his truck. "Is it just me, or does she sound more grown-up every day?"

"It's not just you," his sister-in-law told him, casting an adoring look back at her stepdaughter. He handed her two light bags full of rolls, and she laughed. "I can carry more than that."

"Not while I'm around."

Tilting her head in the way that made him think she saw more than most people, she smiled. "Are you like this with Bekah, too?"

"Like what?" he asked, lifting two large hampers filled with sandwiches from the back of his truck.

"Protective. Considering all she's been through, it must be comforting for her to know you're there for her if she needs you."

"I wouldn't know," he hedged, uncomfortable talking about Bekah with someone else. "I guess you'd have to ask her."

Lily laughed quietly. "Judging by that deer-in-the-headlights look you're wearing right now, you'd rather not have me discussing your relationship with her."

"There's nothing to discuss," he insisted a little more forcefully than he'd intended. "We're friends, and we both enjoy working with the animals here."

Lily didn't press, but there was no way he could miss the feminine smirk that came onto her face the second she turned to unbag the rolls and add them to the platters already on the tables. Since anything he might say now would only make the hole he was in deeper, Drew kept his mouth shut and unloaded the supplies as quickly as he could. On his last trip, he pivoted to find Bekah standing behind him with a cup of lemonade in each hand.

"I came over to get something to drink," she explained, "and I thought you might be thirsty."

"Thanks."

He drained the paper cup and crushed it in his fist. Apparently, his brisk response didn't sit right with her, and he felt terrible when she gave him that hesitant look she'd worn so often when she first arrived in town. "You're welcome."

She turned away, and he felt like a complete heel. His instinct was to reach out and catch her hand, but he knew folks were watching and didn't want to do anything that might embarrass her.

"Bekah." She glanced back, and he winced at the uncertainty clouding those beautiful eyes. Fighting the urge to take her in his arms, he stepped closer to make sure no one else could hear him. "It was real nice of you to think of me."

"You've always been so good to me," she pointed

out in a hushed voice. "I wanted to do the same for you."

"I appreciate that. I guess I'm a little out of sorts today."

"All people can talk about is the fire and us," she confided with a sigh. "The first one is understandable, but I don't get the other."

She'd given a voice to his own frustration, and her bewildered look made him chuckle. "Things are a little slow around town these days. Eventually, something else more interesting will happen, and they'll forget all about us."

She gave him a long, pensive look. "Is that what you want?"

For the second time that morning, he'd been asked a question that he didn't have an easy answer for. Knowing she'd take it wrong if he stalled for too long, he punted. "How 'bout you?"

"I asked you first."

She tipped her chin back with a defiant look, and it hit him that this was the first time he'd seen that kind of reaction from her. He wasn't normally all that cautious when it came to women, but he decided it would be wise to tread carefully with this one. Very carefully. "Yeah, you did. To be honest, I'm not sure what I want."

The hardness in her features eased a bit, giving way to a wry smile. "Neither am I. Where does that leave us?"

"You're the brains, sweetheart," he commented with a grin of his own. "I'm just the muscle."

"I think you're a lot smarter than you let on," she

said in an accusing tone. "You like for people to underestimate you, so they don't expect too much."

Wow, she'd nailed him but good. She had him dead to rights, and he figured he could either growl back like Mike would or laugh and give her credit. Since this was Bekah, he went for the second option. "You got me there. How'd you figure me out so fast?"

"I used to be the same way. Thanks to you, I'm not anymore."

With that, she pivoted on the heel of her work boot and dropped her cup into a trash can on her way toward the baby barn. Drew watched her for a few seconds, marveling at how the terrified runaway he'd met not long ago had evolved into this determined, self-confident woman capable of standing toe-to-toe with him without flinching.

As he strolled over to join the grimy work crew, he felt proud knowing that he'd had something to do with her metamorphosis. But in the next moment, that pride was dimmed by something completely unexpected.

Somehow, when he wasn't paying attention, Bekah had snuck around his usual defenses and gotten firmly under his skin. With Colorado calling to him louder every day, he wasn't in a position to get involved with anyone right now. Especially not someone as vulnerable as Bekah.

It figured, he groaned silently. Just when he was seriously considering leaving Oaks Crossing, he'd stumbled across another very personal reason to stay.

"All right, Bekah," Erin announced after she'd been working for about an hour. "Break time."

"I just got started," she protested, her voice muffled

by the dust mask the very practical Erin had insisted they all wear. "I can go for a little while longer."

Their self-appointed foreman gave her a stern glare. "Not a chance. Normally, I appreciate your work-till-you-drop attitude, but in this case it could be hazardous to your health. The sooner you quit arguing with me and go, the sooner you'll be back."

Bekah had never been treated to this no-nonsense side of Drew's petite sister. She was beginning to see why Erin's three brothers did everything they could to avoid making her angry. "Okay. Half hour, right?"

"And not a minute less. I'm timing you," she added, tapping the large face of a man's analog watch that looked as if it had been through a lot over the years. Since she didn't seem to have a choice in the matter, Bekah gave in and left the wrecked storage barn.

Stepping outside, she took off her mask and had to admit Erin was right about the change of scenery. Bekah didn't realize how the soot and burned chaff had been choking her until she took in a lungful of the crisp autumn air and started coughing. Reaching into a huge tub full of ice and water bottles, she took one out and gratefully swallowed nearly half of it before stopping for a breath.

While she adjusted to the cleaner air, she looked around her at clusters of people who were doing a variety of jobs throughout the site. The pastor, his wife and three of their children were cleaning and refilling water troughs that had been set up outside the main building. Several men she now recognized from church were lugging pails of filthy water out from the main building to dump them into a nearby drainage ditch and fill them in the troughs. They paused just long enough to grab doughnuts from a nearby table, shoving them into their mouths whole before hauling their buckets back inside.

She poured some of her own water into her palm and scrubbed it over her face, grimacing at the diluted charcoal that came off her skin. When she was fairly sure she'd gotten the worst of it, she heard footsteps as someone came up behind her. "Excuse me?"

She turned to find a slender young man in khakis and a blue polo shirt approaching her. His wire-rimmed glasses made him look slightly owlish, and the notepad in his hand was a dead giveaway. "You must be the reporter we heard was coming. The clinic's director, Sierra Walker, is around here somewhere. If you wait here, I'll go find her for you."

"Actually, I'd like to talk to you." Offering a hand and his business card, he introduced himself. "Connor Wells. I cover human-interest stories for a small daily paper in Louisville, and we're always looking for items that will touch our readers and also get some play online. This is exactly the kind of thing folks love to read about."

"A fire that endangered the lives of dozens of helpless animals?" she demanded, furious that anyone would even consider leveraging this tragedy to sell a few newspapers or online ads.

"A possible tragedy that was averted by someone who cares very deeply for those helpless animals," he corrected her with a smile. "From what I've been hearing, you're a real hero."

This was the last thing she needed, Bekah thought, her anger quickly turning to panic. While she felt safer in Oaks Crossing than she had anywhere else, that confidence depended heavily on her being just another resident of this sleepy bluegrass town. While her efforts to promote the clinic's wildlife projects hadn't been enough to alert Richie to where she was currently living, calling any more attention to herself wasn't on her agenda right now. Maybe not ever.

But since Connor was intent on getting a story, she knew she needed to give him something else to snag the attention of his readers. "I did what anyone would have done if they'd been here, so you shouldn't be wasting your time on me. The real news is all these people," she explained, sweeping a hand at the groups of volunteers scattered around the property. "The Kinleys started this rescue center to rehabilitate injured wild animals and find homes for unwanted and abandoned pets. The entire town supports their efforts, and all these folks put their plans for today on hold to come and help us with the cleanup."

"I understand you were the one who called in the alarm," he went on, scribbling as he talked. "Do you live close by?"

You have no idea how close, she thought wryly. Her unusual living arrangements were absolutely none of his business, so she skirted around that detail and did her best to angle his attention back to Oaks Crossing in general. "Yes. I'm new in town, but I can tell you this is a community filled with generous, caring people who pitch in when their neighbors need a hand with something. In this me-first world, that's a real find."

"Me-first world," he echoed with a grin. "I like that. Do you mind if I use it?"

"Be my guest. Just don't quote me, because your story should be about all of us, not one of us."

"That's a terrific attitude, Ms.—"

He trailed off, his questioning look making it clear he was expecting her to fill in the blank. But she wasn't falling for that, and she forced a smile. "My name's not important. The work this center does and the people who support that work are your real story. If you start singling a few of us out from the others, won't that diminish the overall human-interest element for your readers?"

"Good point, but my editor's going to ask who I talked to, and I have to be able to name my sources or she might scrap the whole article. It's not just good exposure for us, but great press for a nonprofit endeavor like this. The more people who know about it, the more donations you'll get to help you rebuild."

She hadn't thought of that. The center had been in dire straits even before the fire. Now, even if Animal Palooza was a raging success, some of that money would have to be used to replace the supplies that had been destroyed. That meant hiring the veterinarian the clinic so desperately needed would have to be delayed. Again.

While she was debating what to do, her newly activated phone chimed with a text alert, and on the screen she saw Drew's name with the message Geek boy okay or should I run him off?

The sarcastic tone made her smile, and she quickly texted back, OK.

Trying to be subtle about it, she glanced around and noticed him not far away, chatting with Cam Stewart about something or other. When she caught Drew's eye, he flashed her one of those cute little-boy grins she'd come to adore. Returning the smile, she screwed up her courage and faced the reporter again. "I'm Bekah Holloway. I'm the kennel assistant and web designer for the center."

"Interesting combination. How do you like working here?"

"It's the best job I've ever had."

"From your earlier comments, I gather you're not from around here. What's it like living in such an out-of-the-way place?"

Lifesaving. Comforting. Fulfilling. All those answers flitted through her mind, but one in particular jumped ahead of them all. "Wonderful."

He nodded, adding the detail to his notes. While he continued asking about the various animals housed there and how they were faring after their ordeal, she was only half listening to his questions. Because during the more personal section of his interview, she'd learned something about herself that hadn't occurred to her before.

She wanted to stay in Oaks Crossing. Whether it made sense or not, she knew that was the right decision for her, not just for now but for the future. Because here, she'd be able to escape her past and begin building the kind of life she'd been longing for since striking out on her own after high school.

And she had Geek Boy to thank for her epiphany. Amazing.

Chapter Eight

Bekah had just finished cleaning the grime off the lobby windows when a cute yellow convertible pulled into the rescue center's gravel parking lot. It had been a week since the fire, and she was finally getting to some of the tasks near the end of what she and Sierra had dubbed The Recovery List. It was slow going, but before long she hoped it would feel as if nothing bad had ever happened.

When Lily opened the driver's door and stepped out, Bekah wasn't surprised to find the cheery car belonged to the equally cheery teacher. Even after long days when most people would be grumpy, Lily was one of the most upbeat people she'd ever come across. With his more reserved personality, Mike didn't seem like the best match for his perky wife.

Then again, Bekah thought as she went to greet her visitor, with her disastrous personal track record, she might not be the best judge of something like that.

"Hi there," she said, opening the door for her. "How are you today?"

"Crazed. The kids always get a little zooey this time

of year, with the holidays coming up soon and all." The assessment was accompanied by a wan smile, but Bekah couldn't help noticing it was still a smile. The woman was incredible.

"I'm sorry to hear that. Can I get you anything?"

"As a matter of fact, yes. Not food," she clarified with a conspiratorial gleam in her blue yes. "A favor."

Bekah couldn't think of anything she wouldn't do for the large, loving family that had taken her in when she needed them most. Nothing legal, anyway. "Shoot."

Lily laughed. "That's funny. You sounded like Drew just now."

"No need to insult me," she joked back, motioning for Lily to have a seat in one of the waiting room chairs. "What did you need?"

"I'm always trying to come up with ways to teach my students things without it coming off like a lesson out of a book. Six-year-olds respond much better to experiences than dry lectures."

"Actually, so do most grown-ups," Bekah pointed out. "How can I help?"

"They've all heard about the fire, and since they know I live at the farm, they keep asking me about it. Do you have any wild animals here now that you could bring into school so the kids can see one up close and learn a little bit about them? Most of them have pets, so I'm hoping to expose them to something they wouldn't be able to keep at home."

"Hmm…someone in a cage would probably work best for that. The kids wouldn't be able to touch it, though."

"That's okay. The principal would prefer it that way, I'm sure. So would the parents."

After sifting through her mental list of animals she cared for every day, Bekah hit on the one that had brought her here in the first place. "What about Rosie, our red-tailed hawk? She's not very big, so her cage would be easy to manage."

"That's perfect," Lily approved with a childlike enthusiasm Bekah envied. "When could you and Rosie come in?"

Panic flared in her throat, and she cleared it before trusting herself to speak normally. "You really should ask Sierra. She's had a lot more experience with educational sessions, and she's much better at that kind of thing than I am."

"But you're the one who found the bird," Lily reasoned. "You're the best person to answer the kids' questions about where she came from and how her rehab is going. Oh, and be prepared for some gory questions about what she eats. These are country kids, so they're well aware of what hawks hunt down for breakfast."

"I don't know, Lily. I've never done anything even remotely like this. What if I'm awful at it, and your students hate the lesson more than if you'd taught them out of a book? The whole thing could easily backfire on you."

"Then we'll try something different next time." Patting her shoulder, the stunningly optimistic teacher smiled. "They're kids, and you'll be introducing them to something most of them have only seen from a distance. I'm confident they'll love you and Rosie."

"What if you're wrong?"

"The sun will still come up the next day," she said

breezily as she stood to go. "It's not life and death. It's show-and-tell."

Reassured, Bekah stood and walked her to the door. "Well, since you put it like that, count me in. Just let me know when you want us."

"I will. Thanks so much for your help." And with a bright, encouraging smile, she was gone.

When she was alone again, Bekah went over their brief conversation, trying to figure out what had just happened to her. Basically, she'd been freight-trained by a slender woman who apparently was even more stubborn than her much larger husband. Maybe that was part of what appealed to him, Bekah mused with a smile. She'd always been criticized for her own obstinate character, so she'd assumed it was an innate flaw in her nature that she had to overcome if she wanted to make a relationship work. Could it be there were men in the world who actually considered it a virtue?

The thought had just flitted through her mind when a dark blue pickup whipped into the lot and parked next to her derelict hatchback. Weird as it seemed, she got the distinct feeling that Drew's sudden appearance was more than a coincidence. When she allowed herself the time to consider how much things had improved for her lately, it had often occurred to her that her life had taken a significant turn for the better the day she met the charming Kentucky farm boy.

Not usually one to believe in destiny, she was beginning to suspect that it was more than an accident that had led her to this picturesque village in the middle of nowhere. While she'd decided that God had led her here to help the rescue center, she couldn't help wondering if He'd also had a more personal reason for it.

Maybe, she thought with a smile, He'd detoured her to Oaks Crossing because it was where she'd finally meet a man who would not only accept her as she was but encourage her to spread her wings.

When Drew strolled through the door holding a beat-up toolbox, he pulled up short when he saw her. "What?"

"What do you mean, what?"

"You're smiling at me, and I haven't even said anything yet. When a woman does that, it usually means something's up."

"Just smiling," she assured him, hoping she sounded casual about the whole thing. The startling possibility was still rattling around in her head, and she wasn't ready to share it just yet. "Did you come by for a reason?"

"I ran into Lily at the house earlier, and she told me about her plan to bring one of the rescued animals into school. It sparked an idea for me, and I wanted to run it past you before I mentioned it to her."

"What did you have in mind?"

"This."

Setting down the toolbox, he tapped something on his phone and called up a video of a wildlife presentation in a classroom. The handler held an enormous barn owl on a leather gauntlet on his arm while he explained the bird's habits and where it liked to make its home. Clearly, it had a broken wing because it sat calmly, blinking its large eyes as it slowly swiveled its tufted head and assessed the circle of breathless elementary-schoolers.

"Rosie's not tame like that," Bekah reminded him. "It wouldn't be safe to take her out in front of all those kids. She'd either hurt someone—" she ticked her index finger "—start flying around in a panic—" she ticked the next finger "—or hurt herself struggling to get loose—" one more finger.

"I know, but wouldn't it be cool to record her visit and put it up on the website you're designing? Pictures are great, but videos like this go viral in a few hours. Think of how much exposure we'd get for the center just by recording something you were going to do anyway."

"There are rules about posting that kind of thing," she pointed out, even though she was warming to the idea. "We'd have to get waivers from the school and the kids' parents."

"Lily can handle that part. You bring the hawk, I'll bring the camera— it'll be awesome. If we like the results, we can think about setting up a webcam out in the baby barn. Everyone who visits loves those little critters. Imagine what a hit they'd be online."

He was so excited, she felt awful that her first instinct was to come up with reasons why his scheme wouldn't work. In truth, it was a fabulous idea, and she didn't want to ruin it by being the one negative voice in the room. But for her, there was more at stake than generating much-needed publicity for the rescue center and the fine work it was doing.

Drew seemed to pick up on her reluctance, and his bright expression dimmed considerably. "You're worried about more than legalities, aren't you? What is it?"

Bekah was torn between being honest with him and keeping her fears to herself. She wasn't used to confiding in anyone, and she hesitated to do it now for fear of sounding paranoid. Then again, being supercautious and keeping her head down was what had kept her safe since leaving Cleveland.

While she hesitated, understanding dawned on his face. "You're worried Richie will find you here. Is that it?"

Grateful that he'd saved her from having to voice it out loud, she nodded. "I told that reporter my name, and I've been regretting it ever since."

Stepping closer, Drew gave her a you-can-count-on-me grin. "I promise, if Richie ever shows his slimy face within ten feet of you, I'll take care of him."

"It's sweet of you to offer, but you don't know what he's like."

"Ornery? Insane? Oh, wait," he went on, eyes twinkling in fun. "He's got two heads. With horns."

Actually, the description wasn't far off of how Richie had appeared in her nightmares. Used to, she added silently. Come to think of it, she hadn't had one of those since the day Drew had handed her the key to her tiny apartment and given her something she'd begun to think she'd never have.

A place to belong.

Gazing up at this wonderful man who'd picked her up off the ground and helped her regain her footing, she sensed something flickering to life inside her. She hadn't felt it in so long, she hardly recognized it, but it felt like hope.

"You still want to be my hero, is that what you're saying?" All on its own, a smile was inching across her face, and this time she didn't bother trying to stop it.

"Well, I'm not exactly Superman, but I'll give it a shot."

"Why?"

"Because I like seeing you smile."

"Oh, you're good," she teased, which was very unlike her. "You probably say that to all the girls."

"Only if it's true."

She noticed he didn't deny that he'd said it before, and she appreciated his honesty more than she could say. A guy as good-looking and thoughtful as Drew must've had dozens of girlfriends over the years, and yet here he was, doing everything he could to make her feel better.

So, because she trusted him to keep his end of their bargain, she put aside her misgivings and decided to take a chance. "Okay, you've convinced me. I'll do the video with Rosie."

"Fantastic!" Hugging her quickly, he held her at arm's length and nearly blinded her with a boyish grin. "This is gonna turn out great for everyone, Bekah. You'll see."

She did her best to return the smile, but in the back of her mind a well-entrenched voice cautioned her that it would be much wiser for her to stick to the shadows and avoid shining a spotlight on herself. She'd been doing that for so long, it had grown from short-term survival technique to long-standing habit.

Living in constant fear wasn't something she relished. Eventually, she knew she'd have to put the past behind her and make a new plan for the future. In this tight-knit community, with Drew and his family supporting her, maybe now was the time.

And if not, she didn't even want to think about how their little experiment would end.

Then she remembered the toolbox he'd brought in with him, and it occurred to her that he must have stopped by for a reason that had nothing to do with Lily's spur-of-the-moment idea. "Did you need something?"

"Came to fix that cranky sliding door Sierra's been harping on me about. I know you've been busy and all, but have you called your insurance company about replacing your windshield?"

"I don't have that kind of insurance," she confessed. "Glass coverage was more than I could afford."

"You and me both," he said in a way that made her feel slightly less pathetic. Opening the front door for her, he went on. "We can probably find one in a junkyard and get it installed for next to nothing. Meantime, I figured we could start with this."

Reaching down, he picked up a can of gas he'd brought with him. It was a large one, and she suspected it held more fuel than she'd been able to buy at any one time all summer long. While things had been going fairly well, she'd tucked away as much money as she could, hoping it would last until she found somewhere to crash for a few months. Then her car had started acting up, and harvest season had drawn to a close, and the safety net she'd so painstakingly scraped together had vanished in a few short days.

Judging by Drew's sympathetic look, he knew all that. Grateful that she didn't have to explain it to him, she forced herself to look on the bright side as they walked over to where her car was parked.

"Gas is expensive these days," she felt obliged to point out. "Let me know how much you gave me, and I'll pay you back."

"Don't worry about it."

She'd learned that his cavalier attitude was part of

his personality, but accepting handouts wasn't going to help her become more independent. "I appreciate the offer, but I already owe you for the mechanic you hired, and now this. I'd feel better if you'd let me pay my own expenses."

"Tell you what," he replied with a slow grin. "Make me dinner sometime."

The suggestion was ludicrous, considering her current living arrangements, and she laughed. "In my gourmet kitchen?"

"I've got a decent setup at my place, so we can get together there. You bring the ingredients, I'll supply the pots and pans."

It sounded cozy, but in the interest of being up-front with him, she hesitated. As tempting as spending an evening with him was, she didn't want to create the impression that there was a possibility for more between them. "I don't know."

"Aw, come on," he wheedled in a practiced tone that told her he'd done it many times before. "I'll even take care of the dishes."

What harm could it do? she wondered, not at all surprised when her well-conditioned mind began making a list of things that had gone awry in the past. But this was Drew, someone who'd been nothing but good to her since their paths had crossed so unexpectedly. Without him, she'd likely still be wandering around Kentucky, searching for a job and a place to live.

Or worse, she'd have come to the conclusion that Richie was right, and she wasn't equipped to make it on her own. As soon as that thought rolled through her mind, she rejected it with a firmness that both startled and impressed her.

She couldn't recall the last time she'd been proud of herself, and she knew the upswing in her perspective was closely tied to the positive things that had happened to her since she found herself in Oaks Crossing. She'd been stuck here because of her car, and she recognized that once the windshield was fixed, she could go anywhere she wanted.

But, to her astonishment, she was no longer keen to leave town the moment she was able. With Drew's promise to shelter her echoing in her ears, she cast aside the last of her reservations and relented with a smile. "Well, since you're willing to wash up, how could I say no?"

"Awesome," he approved, hazel eyes lighting with anticipation. "I should warn you, though, I'm not much of a housekeeper."

"Why am I not surprised?"

"Mom feeds me at the farm most nights, and by the time I get home, I'm so beat, I just go to bed. I don't even have any plants."

Having seen how Maggie doted on her grown children, his account sounded about right to Bekah. "You live close by, then?"

"About a half mile down the road, second driveway on the left. It used to be the farm manager's house, so it's not much to look at, but the price is right."

"Speaking of price," she commented as she glared at her ruined windshield, "how much do you think that will cost?"

"Let's find out." Whipping out his phone, he typed something in and handed it over so she could see the result.

"The tutoring money Sierra's going to pay me will

cover that, and then some," Bekah said, relieved by yet another piece of good news. They were starting to add up, and she was gradually losing her I-can't-believe-it attitude. Flipping Drew's phone over, she admired the sleek design and the sturdy case that protected it from the dirt and knocks he probably subjected it to on a daily basis. "This is nice."

"And easy to use, even for a low-tech guy like me. They've got a deal going right now. Once you pay the monthly charge, the phone's free."

It was the monthly fee that had tripped her up before, which was why her old cell phone was currently a useless paperweight. Living on the razor's edge didn't appeal to her, and she had no intention of ever being that hard off again.

She reluctantly handed the gadget back before she had a chance to get too attached to something she couldn't possibly afford. "Unless you need an extra pair of hands out here, I'll get out of your way."

"You're not in my way," he assured her as he pocketed his phone. He picked up the gas can, and she turned to go. "Bekah?"

Facing him again, she replied, "Yes?"

"God's on your side, and things'll work out the way He means for them to," he told her in a gentle voice. "You'll see."

Not long ago, she'd have politely accepted his kind gesture, knowing in her heart that while he meant well, he was wrong. But now, the tiny hopeful part of her that still existed stood up a bit straighter, wanting to believe. "I hope you're right."

He flashed her an encouraging smile, and she did her best to return it before heading inside. Up until now, he'd been true to his word, and she'd learned that it was safe for her to trust in his honesty. The problem was, her past was something that even God couldn't control.

She dreaded the day that past came crashing down on her like a brick wall, destroying the very fragile existence she'd started to build for herself. Then again, continuing to flee from those demons hadn't worked out, either. Maybe Drew was right, and the time had finally come for her to dig in somewhere and stand her ground. Much as the prospect of confronting her abusive ex-boyfriend terrified her, it was far more appealing to her than running away again.

At least here, she had a steady job and her own place to live. Like Drew had said about his own house, it wasn't ideal, but the price was right.

So, at least for the time being, she'd be staying put. She prayed that someday Richie would be a blip in her memory's rearview mirror, and she'd hardly think about him except to wonder how she'd fallen so far that she'd actually given up control of her life to someone else.

While she checked the clinic's new emails, she took comfort in the fact that she'd emerged from all that turmoil stronger and wiser than she'd been before. For the first time she could remember, she was firmly holding the reins that guided her toward a future that she'd chosen for herself, by herself.

And despite all the uncertainties that still remained for her, it felt wonderful.

Chapter Nine

"And this," Lily said, motioning toward the covered cage, "is the very special guest I was telling you about earlier."

Taking her cue, Bekah whipped away the canvas cover to reveal Rosie, sitting upright on her branch like a soldier at attention. Drew zoomed in to catch the bird's regal pose, then isolated her face, complete with bright eyes that were studying her young audience with hawkish curiosity. For their part, the kids were completely silent, wide eyes glued to the bird in fascination. Or fear. It was hard to tell.

"A few weeks ago, Bekah Holloway found this beautiful hawk injured at the side of the road and took her to the Oaks Crossing Rescue Center," Lily continued, conveniently leaving out the part about the accident. "Now she works there with Rosie and the other animals, helping to get them ready for new homes or to go back into the wild. She's here to tell you about her job and answer questions for you. Quietly and one at a time," she added in the gentle but firm tone Drew recognized from many of her conversations with his big brother.

Muting a grin that would jar the camera's focus, he shifted the lens to Bekah. She looked composed on-screen, but out of the frame he noticed her fingers threaded together so tightly, their knuckles were pale. Fortunately, the kids didn't seem to notice, and she relaxed as she warmed to her subject.

Most of what she told them came straight out of the new flyer she was designing, listing the services the clinic offered, along with their hopes for future expansion. When she was finished, she spread her hands open wide. "Okay, those are the basics. What would you like to ask me?"

Small hands shot into the air, and she called on each kid in turn, answering their questions carefully and honestly. One girl asked, "Are you going to keep Rosie?"

"Oh, no," Bekah replied, shaking her head for emphasis. "She's a wild creature, and she wouldn't be happy living in a cage for very long. We're going to release her later this month, from a clearing in the woods out near the center. The details will be on our new website soon, so if any of you want to come, you can have a grown-up help you find the information there. You and your families are welcome to join us."

Brilliant, Drew congratulated her silently. Folks these days were so wired in, these kids and their parents were probably online every day. Directing them to the newly revamped website was a great way to get the word out that the center was not only expanding, but solidly up-to-date on the latest technology, too.

When she called on a young boy, he said, "Hawks eat mice and stuff. How do you catch those for her?"

Bekah looked him dead in the face and with just the hint of a smile replied, "With cheese."

The kids all laughed, and Lily gave her a subtle "okay" sign. Despite Bekah's concerns that this presentation would be a disaster, Drew thought that she had handled every single question with the perfect blend of sincerity and humor. Knowing how far she'd come from the skittish woman he'd first met on that deserted country road, Drew couldn't have been prouder of her.

When the class finally ran out of questions, Lily stood back up to regain their attention. "All right, guys, that's it for now. Let's give Miss Holloway and Rosie a nice, gentle round of applause."

Somehow, they managed to show their appreciation without spooking the bird, and Drew set the camera on a nearby desk to keep it rolling while he went over to help Bekah wrangle the oversize cage.

"Great job," he murmured as they dropped the canvas into place. "They all loved you."

"It's Rosie," Bekah corrected him with her usual humility. "She's so beautiful and smart, people can't help loving her."

Drew wanted to echo the compliment for her, but he knew she'd just brush it off. Instead, he said, "You both did a terrific job here today. For yourselves and for the center."

After saying goodbye to Lily and her class, they headed out to where he'd parked his truck.

While they got Rosie's cage latched tightly into place, Bekah asked, "Did the video come out okay?

Was I speaking loud enough? My heart was racing so fast, I felt like my voice was shaking the entire time."

"Why don't we head to the clinic and get Rosie settled? Then we can watch the recording and see what you think."

"But what did *you* think?"

"I told you, I thought you did great."

"Sorry," she mumbled, ducking her head in the hesitant old gesture he hadn't missed in the least. "I didn't mean to hassle you."

It hadn't occurred to him that she'd interpret his comment as irritation, and he wanted to kick himself for not being more considerate. This woman had been abused in more ways than he cared to think about. While he'd done everything he could to make her feel safe, what she needed most from him was patience. And after he'd given her that, more patience.

Sneaking his finger under her chin, he gently tipped her face up so she was looking directly at him. He wasn't humble by nature, but he recognized that he'd handled the situation badly, and he wasn't about to let the moment pass without at least trying to make it right. "You weren't hassling me. If what I said gave you that impression, then I apologize."

"Really?" When he nodded, she gave him a wan smile. "Thank you."

"You're welcome. I can be a little dense sometimes, so you'll have to let me know when I screw up. Okay?"

He could almost see the wheels turning in that quick mind of hers, examining his request for some kind of trick. Mistrustful as she was in general, it amazed him that she was standing here, looking him in the eye, discussing something so deeply personal. To his mind, that was progress. For both of them.

Saturday night.

Sprawled out on the sofa in the clothes he'd worn all day, Drew was trying to convince himself to get up and throw some of his mother's leftovers in the microwave. Or take a shower. But so far he'd barely managed to toe off his work boots, listening to them thud on the battered wide plank floor before the house fell silent again.

Pathetic, he scolded himself with all the energy of a snail going uphill. At least the snail had a plan, he thought wryly. Him, he had nothing. And considering how bushed he was, he didn't envision that situation changing anytime soon. Working his usual long hours at the farm and extra time at the rescue center had finally worn him out.

When someone knocked at the front door, he ignored it. After all, the cottage was dark, so if he kept quiet, they might just assume he'd hit the sack early. Then he heard Bekah's voice.

"Drew, I know you're still awake in there. Open the door."

If it had been anyone else standing on his porch, he wouldn't have moved an inch. But since it was Bekah, he hauled himself up off the couch and trudged to the door. Pulling it open, he hung on it with a wan smile. "Hey."

"Wow, you look terrible."

"Thanks for noticing. What'd you need?"

In answer, she held up a large box. "I made you dinner."

"Seriously?" Fingering open the top, he got a whiff of a rich, homey smell that made his mouth water. "Is that what I think it is?"

"Roast beef and potatoes."

Despite his exhaustion, he felt a smile creeping in. "My favorite."

"That's what your mom said when I asked her. I splurged on a slow cooker the other day, and I decided to try it out."

"What's the occasion?"

"There isn't one," she admitted shyly. "I got this month's tutoring fee from Sierra today, and now that I have a new windshield, I didn't need it for anything in particular. Then I remembered that I was supposed to make dinner for you, to pay you back for the gas you put in my car when you came by to make repairs at the kennel."

He almost told her to forget about the debt, then recalled how adamant she'd been about paying what she owed. The fact that she felt confident enough in their friendship to oppose him on something, even something this trivial, was a good sign. "Okay, then. Come on in."

He reached out for the box, but she stubbornly held it out of his reach. "I'll handle this while you go get cleaned up."

"Is that a hint?"

She wrinkled her cute little nose. "I could make it more direct if you want."

"No," he replied with a chuckle. "I get the drift. Help yourself to whatever's in the kitchen. I'll be out soon."

"Sierra's at the clinic doing inventory with some

of our volunteers, so I've got a couple of hours. Take your time."

Drew wasn't a fussy kind of guy, so ten minutes later he was scrubbed from head to toe and had shed his filthy jeans and T-shirt for clean ones. Padding out of the single bedroom in his bare feet, he smelled something that was almost unheard-of in what Mom called his Bachelor Cave: fresh, home-cooked food.

Leaning on the pass-through that went into the living room, Bekah gave him a chiding look. "Your fridge is full of take-out containers and plastic cups."

"Yeah, well, I'm not much of a cook," he confided with a laugh. "I pretty much exist on leftovers and pizza."

"So you're saying I should leave you the extra?"

She was taunting him, and he wondered if this was the same woman who could barely look him in the eye only a few weeks ago. Picking up on her teasing, he retorted, "Only if it's good."

"I guess that depends on how you like your beef. I do a nice peppercorn rub and then simmer it for a few hours in my secret sauce."

She held up a bottle of commercial seasoning, and he laughed. "What a coincidence. That's just how I like it."

"You're not fooling anyone here, farm boy," she informed him, waving a wooden spoon for emphasis. "You'd probably say that no matter what, just to get a free meal."

The meal wasn't what he was interested in, he thought as he strolled through the archway into the kitchen. It was the chef. While it was the absolute truth, he knew she'd probably think he was handing her a well-rehearsed line. So he made a show of looking around and asked, "What can I do to help?"

"I was just hunting up a knife to cut the bread before I warm it in the oven."

She'd given him the easiest, most foolproof job possible, he mused while he dug out the gourmet knife set Erin had given him last Christmas. There was a dusty red bow on top of the box, and Bekah gave him an amused look. "Let me guess. You're not much good in the chopping and dicing department."

"Guilty as charged. My little sister would scream if she knew these things were still in the original box."

"And then some," Bekah added, taking out the shiny slicing blade and washing it off before handing it to him. "You boys must know you drive her completely bonkers."

He just grinned, and she shook her head at him. "That's mean."

"Yeah, but she makes it so easy."

"With Lily in the family now, the balance of power around here is shifting over to the girls. Pretty soon Abby will be old enough to give you a hard time, and you guys will have to start behaving yourselves."

"Don't count on it," he challenged her, snapping the end from a celery stick with his teeth. "Things work fine just the way they are, and we're not likely to change 'em anytime soon."

"We'll see."

Her cryptic response was accompanied by an equally cryptic smile, the kind women wore when they believed they knew significantly more about something than he did. Drew was mulling that over when it occurred to him that she'd implied she'd be around to see his brothers and him get their attitudes adjusted. The idea of her staying in Oaks Crossing appealed to him a lot more than it should have for someone committed to keeping this beautiful, perplexing woman at arm's length.

And then there was Colorado. He still hadn't made up his mind about that, and he knew Nolan couldn't wait much longer.

Eager to get something decided, Drew searched for a way to find out her plans without making it sound as if he was overly invested in her decision. "Y'know, I was thinking earlier that if you're planning to stay in town, you should find a more permanent place to live. That old office isn't heated, and it's gonna get pretty chilly in there come January."

Her eyes narrowed in a suspicious feminine look he recognized immediately, and she pinned him with a hard stare. "What are you getting at?"

"Nothing," he insisted, cutting up the bread as though his life depended on it. "Forget I said anything."

After several incredibly awkward moments of silence, her small hand settled on his, and he stopped slicing. When he looked up, he saw understanding in those soft blue eyes. "Are you trying to ask me when I'm leaving?"

Other women he'd known were much easier to fool, accepting whatever he told them because they didn't bother looking beneath the surface for a deeper meaning. Maybe because it didn't occur to them that he might have another level beyond the one he showed them.

Bekah was a different story altogether, and there

wasn't much point in fencing with her. He'd never win. "Actually, I'm trying *not* to ask you."

"Why?"

"'Cause it's none of my business. If you want to go, you should go."

"What if I want to stay?"

"You should do that, too." He winced at the moronic turn this conversation had taken. Normally, he was smooth and self-assured around women, but right now he reminded himself of Josh, who still got tongue-tied around girls he liked. Giving himself a mental shake, Drew made a desperate attempt to redeem himself. "I mean, you should do whatever makes you happy. You've had a tough time, and you deserve to be happy."

She rewarded him with a heartwarming smile that made him feel slightly less stupid. "That's very sweet. Thank you."

"You're welcome."

Fortunately for him, the oven timer went off, and her attention shifted from him to their dinner. Anxious to put all this foolishness behind him, he quickly laid two place settings on the breakfast bar he used as a table. After rescuing the spare stool from its television-holding duty, he went through the fridge, hoping to find a stray pitcher of something to drink.

"Sorry," he apologized when he came up empty, "but all I've got is water."

"That's okay. I prefer that, anyway."

"Haven't gotten a taste for sweet tea?" he asked as they sat across the counter from each other.

"Not really. I like the strawberry lemonade at the café, though. It's delicious."

Drew tucked that bit of information away for later

and finally thought of asking her about her day. If only he'd done that earlier, he groused, he wouldn't have lost his footing and made a complete idiot of himself.

"Actually," she told him in between bites, "the animals are all doing well. It's the website that's giving me fits."

"Computer problems again?"

"No, I zapped all the viruses, and it's fine now. The problem is I'm not thrilled with the site design, and I've stared at it so long, I can't figure out what's not working. Another set of eyes would really help, but I hate to ask Sierra when she's so stressed about her finals."

"I've got a set of eyes," he reminded her with a grin. "I'd be happy to take a look and give you some unhelpful advice."

That made her laugh, and he realized that he'd been hearing the joyful sound more and more lately. The cloud that had been hanging over her when she'd arrived in town seemed to be losing its grip, leaving a brighter, more optimistic outlook in its place. He wished he could come up with a way to tell her that without making both of them feel uncomfortable, but he couldn't.

Instead, he settled for being practical. "I've got a laptop in the living room. After dinner, we can take a look at the screens you're worried about."

"Are you sure? I mean, you look totally beat."

"You'll be doing the hard part, so I can manage."

A little grin tugged at the corner of her mouth, giving her a playful look he hadn't noticed before. "Do you ever get tired of being my hero?"

"Not so far."

The instinctive reply startled him, but her grateful smile made him glad he'd said it. The connection he felt with her was unusual for him, to say the least. Since Kelly had left, his relationships with women had been either friendly or romantic. Hard as he'd tried, he still couldn't figure out where he and Bekah fell on that scale, and the uncertainty should have scared him to death.

But it didn't. What that meant, he couldn't say. But he had a feeling his nice, quiet little life was about to become very interesting.

Once they were finished eating, he piled the dirty dishes and pans in the sink. When Bekah started the water running, he waved her off. "You cooked, I'll get these."

"When?" she asked, eyeing the stack that constituted a significant portion of the cookware and dishes he owned.

"Tomorrow after church." She gave him a skeptical look, and he laughed. "Really. You can even come back and check to make sure I did it."

"Is that your cool-guy way of inviting me to visit again?"

"Actually, I thought it was pretty straightforward."

"I'm sure."

Her tone was hard to interpret, but the sparkle in her eyes told him he'd hit the right note this time. It wasn't easy with her, but for some reason, he kept on trying. She was the most challenging woman he'd ever met, and not long ago he never would have put in this kind of effort to get to know her. But something kept nudging him forward, convinced that in the end, everything he was doing would be worth it.

"So," he commented, tossing the oven mitts onto the counter by the sink, "let's have a look at the website."

They settled side by side on his hand-me-down sofa and powered up the one high-tech gadget he'd splurged on not long ago: a shiny new laptop. When the screen blossomed into an aerial view of the farm, Bekah said, "Wow. I had no idea how big Gallimore Stables is. What's all this over here?" she asked, pointing to a section of unused land to the east.

"Dad used to call it the Buffer Zone. It's about fifty acres and separates us from the dairy farm in the next valley." Drew looped a finger farther out from the developed acreage, circling all the land the Kinleys owned. "There's a great stream running through it, with trout and bass nearly as big as you are."

That got him another dubious look. "Seriously?"

"They're big," he assured her with a grin. "I'll take you fishing out there sometime. You can bring along a tape measure and judge for yourself."

Gazing at the screen, she commented, "It's really pretty, all wild and untamed like that. I've never spent a lot of time outdoors, but around here everything's so beautiful, it's impossible not to."

"Yeah, I like it, too. We all do," he added quickly to avoid sounding too personal. The moment stretched out awkwardly, and Drew covered his discomfort by handing off the computer. "Take it away."

"Okay, but remember it's still in development. Things aren't polished yet."

"Gotcha."

After a few quick keystrokes, she opened up the new website she'd been designing for the center. The first thing he noticed was that she'd found a way to reproduce their logo, which arched over the center of each page to give them all a cohesive look. She clicked through various sections, explaining what was there and what she wanted to add.

When she got to the video section, an idea popped into his head. "We still have to put that webcam in the baby barn."

"I totally forgot," she commented, clicking over to a digital notepad to add the suggestion, along with one about uploading the video of Rosie's school visit. "We just have to buy a webcam and mount it in there."

"I don't think they cost much. If we do more than one, people could pick which kind of animal they want to watch."

"We could even put them in the puppy and kitten areas," she suggested brightly. "Once people see how adorable they are, they'll get adopted faster."

"No doubt."

While they kicked ideas around for improving certain sections of the site and adding things that weren't there yet, Drew felt himself warming to the project. Normally, he was a hands-on kind of guy, and brainy pursuits like this didn't hold much appeal for him. But cozied up on the couch with this unexpectedly creative woman, he was surprised to discover that he didn't mind using his head for a change.

Just another aspect of his life that had changed since he met Bekah, he mused with a grin. Who could've guessed that while he was trying to improve her life, she'd end up doing the same for him?

Monday morning was unreal.

Bekah stood at the counter in their freshly scrubbed

lobby, opening email after email inquiring about how to donate to the rescue center's rebuilding fund. Many of the locals who'd come to help with the cleanup had not only given their time and effort, but left behind checks and cash whose total still blew her mind. With Animal Palooza right around the corner and people from outside Oaks Crossing interested in donating, the center just might earn a much-needed sense of financial security.

All that generosity showed Bekah what could be accomplished when a bunch of regular people came together and devoted their energies to a common cause. It was a good lesson for someone like her to learn, and she'd taken it very much to heart.

The phone rang, and the caller ID told her it was Sierra. "Morning, boss. How's your cram session going?"

"Long and tedious. I think my eyes are starting to cross, so I decided to take a break. How're things there?"

"Do you want the good news or the good news?"

The center's director answered with something between a yawn and a laugh, and Bekah explained. "We got another set of donations in this morning's mail, and more emails from folks asking what we still need. As if that wasn't enough, our new media pages are trending online. It's unbelievable."

"That fire might turn out to be a blessing in disguise. Erin and I were looking over the books last night, and if Animal Palooza brings in the crowd we're expecting based on the number of RSVPs, it seems like we'll be able to afford to keep you on after the end of the year. If you want to stay, that is."

For once, Bekah didn't hesitate, buying time to consider all the possible angles and how things could go wrong. Delighted by the offer, she quickly said, "I love working here, so I'd be thrilled to stay on. Thank you so much."

"You've totally earned it, but you're welcome. I'm hoping we can give you a raise, but Erin and I will have to do the year-end books to make sure."

"What I'm making now is fine," Bekah assured her, smiling even though no one was there to see it. "If you've got extra money floating around, use it to get a top-notch veterinarian in here."

"See? That's what I love about you."

They were both laughing when the front door opened, and Bekah glanced up to see who'd come into the lobby.

Abruptly, she stopped laughing and stared at the man who'd been the star of her worst nightmares for months. Richie raised his hand in greeting, then folded his arms in a clear message that he was willing to stand there and wait until she talked to him.

Bekah's heart leaped into her throat, and she swallowed hard to force it back to where it belonged. Taking a deep breath to steady her voice, she said, "Sierra, I have to go. We'll talk more later."

"What's wrong?"

"Nothing. Something just came up that I have to handle. I'll call you back."

She hung up before Sierra could say anything more and faced her unwelcome visitor with a grim expression. "Richie."

"Bekah." Glancing around, his dark eyes settled on her with an approving look. "It looks like I was wrong."

She wasn't falling for that. A few months ago, she

might have taken his admiration at face value, but she was stronger now, more confident. His talent for deception was epic, and the woman she'd become no longer trusted him. "About what?"

"That you couldn't make it without me. It doesn't happen often, but I have to say I'm pleased to be proven wrong."

He moved a few steps closer, and she was grateful to have the sturdy oak counter as a buffer between them. "How did you find me?"

"You can find just about anything on the internet these days."

Of course, she moaned silently. Between the media campaign for the clinic and the article Connor had written, her name was out there for the public to see if they knew where to look. The thought that Richie would somehow locate her had once nearly paralyzed her with fear. Now that he was here, she realized this little reunion would have happened sooner or later, even without the online exposure.

Summoning the spunk that Drew had admired so many times, she faced her ex with a stern expression. "Well, here I am. What do you want?"

"What I've always wanted. You."

He reached out for her hand, and she jerked it away, glaring at him for all she was worth. "I'm not interested."

"But I came all the way from Cleveland to see you," he wheedled, some of the obstinance she remembered slithering into his fond expression. "The least you can do is hear me out."

"I don't think so."

In the time it took her to blink, he grabbed her arm

and yanked her partway over the counter. "You have something that belongs to me, and I want it back."

"I have no idea what you're talking about," she stalled, groping around the shelf hidden behind the facade, praying to find something she could defend herself with.

And then, out of nowhere, Drew appeared behind Richie and tossed him halfway across the lobby as if he was a rag doll. Standing between him and Bekah, Drew planted his hands on his hips and scowled at their unwelcome guest. "You heard the lady. Time to go."

"I don't know who you think you are," Richie protested, shaking off the manhandling with a violent look. "But this is strictly between Bekah and me."

Drew didn't say a word, but he took a single menacing step forward. Even though they were about the same size, Richie backpedaled toward the door. She'd never seen him look frightened before, and it occurred to her that very few people had ever challenged him the way Drew was doing now.

"All right, I'm going, but I'll be back later when your Doberman isn't around." Tossing a business card on the counter, he added, "You know why I'm here, and I'm not leaving until I have what I came for. Call me when you're ready to talk."

"You're wasting your time and your breath," she shot back, pleased to see him shrink away from her for a change. "Go home, Richie. I've got nothing to say to you."

Leveling a furious look at Drew, Richie carefully maneuvered around him and out the door. When his car was out of sight, Drew turned to her with a grim expression. "You okay?"

"Yes." Giving him a wry grin, she lifted the heavy industrial stapler she held in her shaking hand. "He should thank you. You saved him from a beaning."

Her rescuer laughed, eyes twinkling proudly as he came around the counter. "Good for you. When I saw him grab you, it was all I could do not to put him through the wall."

"Then we'd just have more to fix," she teased, able to joke now that her pulse was dropping back into its normal range. "But it's nice to know you would've done something like that for me."

The grin he was wearing mellowed into something else, and his gaze warmed considerably. "Haven't you figured it out yet, sweetheart? I'd do anything for you."

"I—what?" she stammered, mesmerized by the emotion simmering in those hazel eyes.

"You've been under my skin since the first day I met you," he murmured, drawing her into his arms with a lazy smile. "Stuff like that never happens to me."

She'd have given just about anything for a witty comeback, but the best she could scrape up was a meek, "Really?"

"Uh-huh. Why do you think that is?" She mutely shook her head, and he rested his forehead on hers with a heavy sigh. "I'm hoping you can help me figure it out before it drives me crazy."

"Umm…okay."

Pulling his head back, he gave her another one of those heart-skipping grins he seemed to pull out at the best possible times. Brushing a kiss over her lips, he murmured, "I'd appreciate that."

What she'd appreciate was another kiss, although she couldn't summon the nerve to ask him for one.

Somehow he picked up on what she was thinking, and as usual he didn't disappoint her.

Cuddled against him, she let out a deep, contented sigh. "This is nice."

"Yeah, it is."

Her brain finally shifted back into gear, and she tipped her head back to give him a curious look. "How did you know I was in trouble?"

"Sierra," he explained with a grimace. "She didn't like the way you sounded when you hung up with her, so she called me to come and check on you."

"I'm glad she did, but I'm sorry to drag you away from the farm in the middle of the morning this way."

Clearly unconcerned, he shrugged. "No big deal. That endless pile of logs isn't going anywhere."

"Cutting or stacking?"

"Both. I lost the rock-paper-scissors deal, so I got stuck with restocking the firewood for the house." He gave her a sheepish grin that was very unlike him. "Not that I'm complaining or anything. I could be strapped to a chair behind a desk or something."

Bekah tried to picture him dressed in a suit and tie, working in an office, but even her vivid imagination couldn't make the jump. "I can't see you doing the executive thing."

"Yeah, me neither." Understanding glimmered in his eyes, and he added, "Is that what Richie does?"

"Believe it or not, he's the general manager of a high-end department store."

"With his people skills?" Drew scoffed.

"I know—weird, right?"

"Very." He looked out the front window and frowned. "I think I just saw him drive by. He slowed down, then sped up when he saw my truck was still here."

Now that she'd faced him down and survived, Bekah felt more annoyed than threatened by the fact that he hadn't truly left. "What a pain. It's not like I can go somewhere to get away from him. It's almost critter lunchtime, and I'm the only one here."

"Hang on a sec." Pulling out his phone, Drew hit a button and began talking. "Hey, Harley. I need a favor. No, this time it's legit. There's a guy lurking around the center who's not exactly friendly, and Bekah's out here by herself. I'm not sure if he's staying in the area or not, but could you and the other deputies keep an eye out for him? Here's his license plate number."

After he'd rattled it off, he listened for a minute. "I don't think she wants to make a formal complaint at this point, but if he comes around again, she might change her mind. Thanks, man."

Once he'd hung up, Bekah looked at him in amazement. "You got his license plate number?"

"Sure. I watch those detective shows, too, y'know."

He was just full of surprises, this easygoing country boy who'd stepped between her and trouble so many times, she'd lost count. "You probably solve the crimes before the characters do."

"Sometimes."

"Which means most of the time," she corrected him, wrapping her arms around his waist with a playful grin. "Most people would crow about being that smart. How come you're so modest?"

"No need to rub it in, I guess," he replied, ticking the tip of her nose with his finger. "As long as you know the truth, that's good enough for me."

His playful tone gave way to a more serious look, and she held her breath, waiting to see what this remarkable man wanted to tell her.

"Most folks don't bother looking beyond the obvious to what's underneath," he said quietly. "But you do. Why is that?"

"Maybe because I know how it feels to be judged on appearances instead of what really counts." Resting her hand on his chest, she smiled. "What's in here is what makes a person who they are. The rest is just window dressing."

"Does that mean Richie's like a mannequin in a display?"

She considered that for a moment before nodding. "I didn't realize it before, but he's definitely all flash and no substance. That's probably why he can be so mean. He knows he's missing something inside, but he doesn't know what it is so he drags people down to his level to make himself feel better."

"Are you trying to make me feel sorry for the jerk who used to beat you?" Drew demanded with narrowed eyes. "'Cause I can promise you it ain't gonna happen."

Unlike the vows her troublesome ex had made to her over and over, Bekah knew that Drew meant those terse words with every ounce of energy he had. Tears of gratitude sprang into her eyes, and she cuddled into the haven of those strong, sheltering arms that had not only kept her from harm, but had lifted her from her dark past and into a brighter future.

"In the meantime," he continued in a determined voice, "till we're sure he's gone, I'll leave my truck here and hike back to the farm. That way, if he does another drive-by, he'll assume I'm still here and hopefully keep his distance. Do me a favor, though."

"What's that?"

He pointed to the door. "Make sure that stays locked. If you're doing something out back or in the office, I don't want him sneaking up on you."

"But what if a customer comes by?"

"They can ring the bell, like the plaque tells them to. Trust me. No one wants you putting yourself in danger just because the sign on the door says Open."

His borderline paranoia about her safety probably wasn't necessary, but she couldn't fault him for being overly cautious. Knowing she didn't have to cope with this new challenge on her own gave her the same warm, cherished feeling she'd had the night of the fire when he'd held her this way. Whether she was at her worst or her best, he'd been a constant source of strength and comfort for her since the day she blundered into his hometown, lost and alone.

Even though it didn't seem like nearly enough to repay him for all he'd done, she gave him her biggest, brightest smile. "Thank you, Drew."

"For what?"

"For always being there for me, no matter what. You're my everyday hero."

"Everyday hero," he echoed with that crooked grin she'd come to treasure. "I likc the sound of that."

"I thought you might."

Chapter Ten

"I love Monday night football," Drew announced as he sprawled out on the living room floor at the farmhouse. "What a great way to start the week."

"It doesn't have anything to do with Cincinnati being favored by two touchdowns over Oakland, does it?" Erin teased, tossing a fluffy piece of popcorn at the back of his head.

"'Course not. I just love the game."

Josh was sitting next to him and slid a little farther away. When Drew gave him a questioning look, he explained, "For when the lightning bolt comes to strike you down."

"I'm totally serious."

Mike barked out something that could have been laughter. "Since when?"

"I'm always serious about football."

Glancing over his shoulder, he winked at Bekah. That made her laugh, and he was relieved to hear it. Richie's stunt had clearly unnerved her, and about ten minutes after Drew had left the clinic earlier, he'd put off his long list of neglected barn chores to spend the rest of his day there to make sure she wasn't alone.

Not only was he concerned about her personally, he didn't believe for a second that a controlling, domineering guy like Richie had come all this way to bring her back with him and would now meekly turn tail and go home without her. Men like him simply weren't wired to be cooperative. Even when it was in their own best interests.

Beyond that, he couldn't forget Richie's parting shot.

You know why I'm here, and I'm not leaving until I have what I came for.

Drew had patiently waited all day for Bekah to offer some kind of explanation, but he still had no clue what her ex was talking about. Apparently, she was content to ignore it and go on as if nothing unusual had happened.

But he wasn't.

While they all debated the pluses and minuses of Cincy's new quarterback, Drew subtly kept an eye on Bekah. She seemed to be following their conversation, but her troubled eyes kept flicking to the open screen door with a view up the driveway to the road that led past the farm. Drew would've given anything to be able to tell her that Richie was gone for good and she was safe now.

But much as he wanted to reassure her, he drew the line at lying to make her feel better. Not only was it wrong, but she'd see right through it. He'd worked hard to earn her trust, and he wasn't about to do anything that would cause her to withdraw back into the shell she'd been in when he first met her.

So he settled for catching her eye and giving her what he hoped came across as a confident grin. She responded with a tentative smile, but the gratitude shining in her eyes balanced it out. Under the circumstances, he figured that was about the best he could ask for.

The game was a defensive battle, and just before halftime, the teams were tied at seven. During a commercial, Drew strolled into the kitchen to get a soda from the fridge.

Erin sat at the large table, staring wide-eyed at something on her laptop. When she noticed him, she motioned toward the screen. "Bekah did an amazing job on the new website. It's so fabulous, I can't even remember what the old one looked like."

"Tell her that, wouldya?"

"Absolutely."

Shouting erupted from the front parlor, and he grinned. "Parker likes his new game?"

"He taught Abby how to play, and they're having a blast. It's giving me some time to get caught up with clinic business." Leaning back in her chair, she gave him the Mom look that must have come with the ream of foster-parent papers she'd signed when she took in Parker. "You've been acting worried all night, which isn't like you at all. What's going on?"

"Wish I knew," he confided, perching on the end of a long bench. He nutshelled what he'd seen and heard during the day, ending with "She won't tell me the whole story, and I'm afraid if I ask her directly, she'll think I'm prying. What should I do?"

"Send her in here," Erin suggested immediately. "I'll find out."

"I don't know. That sounds like a bad idea."

She waved that off like a gnat. "It's girl talk. I'll start out giving her notes on the website, then move over to what Sierra told me about that weasel showing up unannounced. If there's something you need to know, I'll share."

"Who decides if I need to know?"

"Me." Raising one eyebrow, she added an evil grin. "Take it or leave it."

"Anything else?" Bekah asked, pen poised over her notepad to record more input from the woman Sierra affectionately called The Boss. She hadn't had much direct contact with Erin before the fire, but since then they'd bonded over their mutual concern for the animals and how to approach bringing the clinic's facilities back up to speed.

"Not that I can think of."

Bekah eyed her notes dubiously. "Are you sure? This isn't very much to fix."

To her surprise, the usually serious Erin laughed. "That's because you did such a great job. Take the compliment, okay?"

"Okay. Thanks."

"You're welcome." After a sip of fragrant orange tea, Erin leaned back and gave her a long, assessing look. "A little birdie mentioned that you had a less-than-welcome visitor at the center today. Tell me about it."

It wasn't a request, Bekah noticed wryly. It was an order from someone who was accustomed to people obeying her—either out of love or fear. And judging by the patient expression she was wearing, she fully intended to sit at this table until Bekah answered the question to Erin's satisfaction.

Bekah wasn't used to people troubling themselves about her well-being, and a few weeks ago the prying would have sent her scurrying back into the shadows to avoid calling attention to herself. Now, though, she took the meddling as proof that Erin not only cared about her, but would help if she could. "What did Drew tell you?"

"The basics, but I think he's missing the big picture. You left Cleveland months ago, so I want to know why Richie would put so much effort into hunting you down in the first place."

Bekah had kept the truth to herself for so long, it felt like a part of her. But as she met Erin's direct, unflinching gaze, she realized the time had come to share it with someone who just might be able to help her shed the past once and for all.

"Before I tell you the gory details, let me ask you something." Erin nodded for her to continue. "You work for a judge, right?"

"I'm his office assistant, not a paralegal. Why?"

"I have something that needs to stay safely tucked away, but I'm not sure it's legal to do that and I don't want to cause you any ethical problems."

Erin leaned in and spoke more quietly. "Something of Richie's?"

"Not exactly." Bekah considered what she was about to do one more time, then took a deep breath and forged ahead. "The department store I used to work at went bankrupt just before I left Cleveland. I have evidence that proves it was mostly because Richie and the senior accountant were embezzling money from the company."

Erin's eyes rounded in shock, and Bekah almost expected to be accused of participating in the crime. She was relieved when Erin said, "Those crooks. A lot of people must've lost their jobs because of what those two did."

"More than a hundred of them, from maintenance to upper-level managers. I didn't know what was going on until the end, when Richie left some of the undoctored financial reports at the apartment. When I realized what they were, I realized he was more than abusive—he was a criminal. I knew that if I didn't get out of there, people would assume I was in on their scheme, and I'm sure he wouldn't tell them otherwise."

"That's awful," Erin seethed. "You could've ended up in jail."

"In a heartbeat. I had no intention of letting that happen, so I copied the computer files onto a portable drive and one day when he was out, I left."

"Good for you," Drew's voice approved from behind her. When she turned, his jaw was set in grim lines that would have frightened her if she didn't know his gentle nature as well as she did. "So that's why he's really here. It's got nothing to do with wanting you back."

"Oh, I don't doubt he misses having me to kick around," she retorted crisply. "But he's a lot more worried about what I know and how I might use it against him."

"What do you need from me?" Erin asked in a pragmatic tone that was oddly comforting.

"Just a safe place to keep the evidence I have. Taking it to the police wouldn't help save the company at this point, but it could put Richie and that crooked accountant away for a long time. I think they'd prefer to avoid that," she added with a wry grin.

Strolling into the kitchen, Drew spun a chair around and sat down. "I know that look, Bekah. You've got a plan."

"I do," she confirmed, glancing from one Kinley to the other. "But I'm going to need a little help."

"I don't like this," Drew muttered to Bekah when they arrived at the Oaks Café the following afternoon. "Have I mentioned that?"

"Repeatedly." Taking his hand, she gave him a confident smile. "I appreciate the moral support, but I don't want you and Richie getting into a fight. Cam promised to keep an eye on me, so you'll have to be content hanging out in the snack bar."

His eyes wandered through the connecting archway, then settled back on her. "I'm gonna sit in view of the door. If he so much as looks at you funny…"

"I know, you'll do terrible things to him. He's due here anytime now, so you need to get going." She gave him a playful shove toward the adjoining room and couldn't help laughing when he didn't budge. "Drew, I'll be fine. I have a plan, remember?"

"Yeah, I remember. I still don't like it."

"Too bad. This is my problem and my solution. Now go." He remained stubbornly by her side, and despite the serious reason she was here, she couldn't help smiling at the sweet, protective gesture. "Please?"

"Well, since you said *please*." Giving her a lopsided grin, he quickly kissed her before walking away.

Bekah had to admit, knowing he was on the other

side of the wall ready to spring into action made her feel a lot more confident than she would have otherwise. She chose a table in the middle of the dining room, in full view of everyone there. Including Cam, who caught her eye from the front desk and gave her a nod.

Despite the ugly confrontation that was probably coming, she'd never felt safer in her life.

When Richie appeared in the entryway, she sent up a heartfelt prayer for courage to carry through with the maneuver she'd so carefully plotted out. While she didn't really expect him to harm her in front of so many witnesses, she wouldn't put it past him to try something more subtle but just as unnerving.

As she watched him come toward her, an unexpected sensation washed over her, replacing her anxiety with a calmness so complete, she felt it all the way to her toes. And in that moment, she knew that if she just followed the course she'd chosen, everything would be all right.

"Hello, Bekah." When he noticed the two chairs were directly opposite each other, he chuckled as he sat. "Was this your idea or your Doberman's?"

"This is a table for two," she replied smoothly. "The chairs are always set up like this."

"Okay, have it your way." Folding his hands on the table, he skewered her with a sharp stare. "I have to admit, I'm impressed."

The compliment caught her off guard, but she managed to maintain contact with those dark, penetrating eyes. "With what?"

"That you called me instead of sneaking out of town in the middle of the night. It's not your style."

"I don't run from my troubles anymore," she informed him icily. "I stand up to them."

"Good for you."

His words echoed Drew's from the night before, but the mocking tone was decidedly different. But now, rather than making her feel small, his condescending attitude just annoyed her. Batting away her irritation, she got down to business. "I have a solution to our mutual problem."

Something akin to respect flared in his eyes. "I'm listening."

"I have proof of what you did to our former employer. It's safely tucked away, with instructions on what to do with it if anything happens to me. It will stay that way as long as you never contact me in any form ever again."

She had his full attention, and she could almost see the wheels spinning in his devious mind. "And if I don't agree to your little blackmail scheme?"

"I'll file restraining orders against you in every state and go to the district attorney with everything I have. When the evidence I've accumulated comes out, you and your numbers guy will be sent to prison for a very long time."

The boldly specific legal threats had been Erin's idea, and while Bekah wasn't certain she could actually follow through on them, she thought they had a nice, official ring to them. Once Richie had a chance to absorb that, she leaned in and added the kicker. "If you want to stay out of jail, all you have to do is leave me alone."

"How do I know you have what you say you have?"

She'd anticipated the challenge, and she slid a few sheets of paper across the table. "These are some random printouts from hundreds of electronic pages. See for yourself."

While he skimmed them, she casually lifted her water for a sip. Cam traded a look with someone in the distance, and she assumed it was some kind of silent communication between him and Drew. Knowing they were watching out for her made her feel all warm and fuzzy inside, and she swallowed a grin that would only have made Richie angry.

"Fine," he spat, tossing the pages back at her. "But how do I know you'll keep your word?"

"Would you like it in writing?" This wasn't exactly the kind of arrangement you documented, and she was more than happy to point that out to the man who'd made her life so miserable for so long.

Apparently realizing he'd stepped into that one, he frowned and shook his head. "No, but you're treading a fine line here. How do I know you'll keep your end of the bargain?"

"You don't," she said evenly. "You'll just have to trust me."

Clearly, he didn't like that, but she had him in a corner, and they both knew it. He stood up and glared down at her. "Like you're going to trust me?"

"I don't have to," she informed him sweetly, waving the papers for emphasis. "This time, I've got all the cards."

Without another word, he pivoted on his heel and stalked from the café. He hadn't been gone more than a few seconds when Drew came over and settled into the vacant chair on the other side of the table. Taking her hands, he pinned her with a worried look. "You okay?"

"I am now."

And for the first time in a very long time, she meant it.

Chapter Eleven

Today was the day.

After weeks of preparation and nervously crossing off the days on their countdown calendar, praying they'd be ready in time, Animal Palooza was finally here. Bekah woke up long before the sun, cleaning and arranging things before going through the clinic's morning routine as efficiently as humanly possible. The critters were more cooperative than usual, which helped tremendously. Then she took another tour, making sure everything was ready for the onslaught of visitors they'd have throughout the day.

When she was satisfied that everything was in the best shape that could be expected, she headed for the area that was quickly gaining fame as their Birds of Prey sanctuary. Long ago, she'd gotten over what they ate for breakfast, but this morning she felt a knot starting to form in the pit of her stomach. Pausing in front of Rosie's enclosure, she rested her palms on the outside of the bars and stared in at the magnificent creature that had inadvertently brought her to the rescue center so many weeks ago.

If it hadn't been for the wounded hawk, Bekah was fairly certain she'd still be on the run, constantly looking over her shoulder instead of in this charming town, working at a job she loved.

"I know this doesn't make any sense to you," Bekah whispered as her eyes welled with tears, "but I'd still be lost if it wasn't for you. I'll never forget you, Rosie."

The bird cocked her beautifully sculpted head and squawked softly. Crazy as it seemed, Bekah couldn't help thinking the bird had understood what she'd said and replied in her own way.

Hanging on to the bars, Bekah closed her eyes, trying to stem her tears. She'd known all along that one day, Rosie would go back to the wild skies where God meant for her to be. But it had always been at some point in the nebulous future. Now it was today, and thrilled as she was for her hawk friend, Bekah couldn't deny that she was going to miss her terribly.

Behind her, a door closed, and she heard familiar boot steps coming up behind her. When Drew's arms came around her, she gratefully turned into his embrace.

"It's stupid," she mumbled into his soft flannel shirt. "I knew she was going to be leaving someday."

"It's always hard to let go of someone we care about, even if we know it's gonna happen."

Bekah angled her head to look into the cage again and let out a deep sigh. "I'm happy for her, though. She's strong and healthy, and it's time for her to go home."

"She's got pretty distinctive markings," Drew said quietly, kissing the top of Bekah's head. "It wouldn't surprise me that if you keep your eyes open, you'll see her around."

Tilting her head back, Bekah smiled up at the kind, generous man who'd done so much for her. "That makes me feel a lot better. Thank you for thinking of it."

"Anything for you," he assured her, sealing his promise with a quick kiss.

"You really mean that, don't you?"

"Wouldn't say it if I didn't."

Gazing into those warm hazel eyes, she felt the depth of that truth with a conviction she'd never experienced with anyone else. Drew had come to mean more to her than she could have dared to hope for, and into her mind came the words that would best tell him how she felt.

"I love you, Drew."

A slow grin drifted across his tanned features. "You do?"

"Yes." More than a little surprised by his reaction, she laughed. "Don't tell me you've never heard that before."

"Too many times," he confided with a grimace. "Usually right before things got ugly and fell apart."

She could only recall a handful of times she'd seen him being anything other than optimistic, and the current of doubt in his voice definitely got her attention. "Are you worried that's going to happen with us?"

"You really feel like there's an 'us'?" he asked, clearly amazed. When she nodded, the grin came back even brighter than before. "That's awesome, 'cause I'm pretty sure I love you, too."

"Pretty sure?" she echoed, giving him a mock glare.

Obviously, he'd caught on that she was teasing, because he laughed as he pulled her closer. "Y'know, when you get mad, those pretty eyes of yours spark like fireworks."

He dropped in for a long, leisurely kiss that she honestly wished could have gone on forever. Unfortunately, the rest of the staff would be arriving any minute, and she reluctantly untangled herself from his arms. "We've got a lot to do today. Why don't we make dinner at your place tonight to celebrate?"

"The fund-raiser or us?"

"Both."

"Sounds good to me."

He drew her in, plainly angling for another kiss, and she pushed him away with a laugh. "The food or the celebrating?"

"Both," he echoed her, eyes twinkling with mischief as he turned and headed for the door that led out to the side yard.

When he was gone, she glanced over at Rosie with a dreamy sigh that was totally unlike her. "Isn't he incredible?"

Bobbing her head, the hawk squeaked her opinion before getting back to preening her feathers. Their exchange made Bekah smile, and she decided it was best to leave now before her melancholy mood rushed back in and ruined the moment.

Before much longer, she was far too busy to think about anything but welcoming visitors, directing them to the various areas they were most interested in, and answering a million questions about everything from what alpacas ate to where the bathrooms were.

She was in the middle of delivering a Puppy 101

lecture to a family adopting an adorable beagle when Sierra came up and put a hand on her shoulder. She didn't say anything, but the understanding look on her face said it all: it was time.

"So, guys," Bekah said, forcing a smile and a chipper tone. "We'll have this little cutie-pie all ready for you before you head home. If you want to get a good spot for seeing our red-tailed hawk take off, you should get outside and find a place along the back fence rail by the woods."

Suddenly, her feet felt like they were made of lead, and they dragged a little slower on every step between the kennel and the large birds area. To her great relief, Drew was already there, lifting Rosie's temporary home onto a wheeled cart. Clearly, he meant to be right beside her when her beloved feathered friend took off, and if there hadn't been a dozen other people milling around the barn, Bekah would have kissed him on the spot.

He really was her everyday hero, she mused for the countless time. Not only because of his down-to-earth manner, but because he was there for her day in and day out, ready for anything that came along.

Because he loved her.

That comforting thought buoyed her sagging spirits, and even though she knew he could manage the cart on his own, she put her hand on one side of the large handle and smiled up at him. "Okay. Let's go send our girl back into the wild blue yonder where she belongs."

He gave her an encouraging smile, and together they hauled the cage out the back door toward the woodsy area their wildlife rehabilitator had chosen for the release. A quick glance showed Bekah a huge crowd had assembled along the rail near the clearing, along with the visionary reporter Connor Wells, who'd returned as promised for the big day. In the past, being presented with all those people would have sent her running for cover. But today, Bekah proudly marched forward, delighted to see that so many folks had turned out to support the rescue center and the critical work it was doing for creatures large and small.

When they had Rosie's cage in place, Sierra climbed onto a picnic table and held up her hands to get everyone's attention. After they quieted, she greeted them with a huge smile. "On behalf of the entire staff of the Oaks Crossing Rescue Center, I want to thank all of you for spending part of your Saturday here with the animals. After our recent fire, I wasn't sure we'd be ready for business anytime soon, so I'd like to get a round of applause for everyone who helped us get back on our feet and those of you who will be contributing to our cause in the future. Thanks to your donations of time and funds, we'll be able to continue fostering animals for many years to come."

The gathering erupted into enthusiastic clapping and cheering, punctuated by several whoops from the Kinley clan standing with Erin near the back. Her delighted expression showed just how much this day meant to her, and Bekah felt honored to be a part of it.

"And now," Sierra called out, "I'd like you to join us in saying a fond farewell to Rosie the red-tailed hawk."

She jumped down and picked up a leather gauntlet she'd left on the table. Then, to Bekah's astonishment, Sierra held the heavy glove out to her. Completely stunned by the offer, Bekah glanced at Drew, but he grinned and shook his head.

"This is your show, sweetheart. You saved her. You should be the one to set her free."

So, because she couldn't come up with a polite way to refuse, she pulled on the gauntlet and eased open the door of the cage. Rosie eyed her with interest and cautiously stepped onto her protected hand. Bekah gently clamped the hawk's talons to keep her under control on her way through the opening. For a brief moment, the two of them locked gazes, and the bird cocked her head in the intelligent pose that made Bekah think that birds were a lot smarter than most folks gave them credit for.

And then, Bekah lifted her into the air, and with a few beats of her strong wings, she was gone. Climbing into the cloudless November sky, she did a few lazy loops overhead and then disappeared from sight behind the trees.

As the crowd cheered their approval, Bekah didn't register that she was crying until Drew put an arm around her for a quick hug. "Man, she was beautiful soaring around up there."

Wiping away tears, she did her best to smile. "She looked happy, didn't she?"

"Yeah, she did." Taking Bekah's shoulders, he gently turned her to face him. "You okay?"

"I will be. We've got a beagle going home with a new family today, and another's on the fence about a pair of kittens. With all these people here, Sierra's hoping to clean out the kennels in the next week or so."

"Sounds doable to me. Who doesn't like puppies and kittens?" Holding out a hand for her, he gave her a confident grin. "Let's go make it happen."

His upbeat attitude was contagious, and her own spirits rose in response. They worked their way through the crowd, answering more questions and planting pet suggestions in people's heads. While they mingled, she was impressed by the easy way he dealt with everyone, making them feel as if they were his friends even if he'd never met them before.

That was Drew, she thought fondly. Handsome as he was, his other qualities were even more special to her. His confidence and quick wit, not to mention his willingness to put in extra effort when he felt that it was necessary.

His great big wonderful heart. If there was another man on the planet she could possibly love as much as this lanky Kentucky farm boy, she couldn't imagine him.

That evening, Drew and Bekah were making lasagna when his cell phone rang. It was Nolan, and he knew it was finally time to fish or cut bait. "That's my buddy Nolan, who lives in Denver. I really should talk to him."

"Go ahead and answer it," she told him while she closed the oven door. "We've got a while before it's ready."

He put the phone on speaker, figuring she had as much right to hear this conversation as he did. "Hey there. I'm guessing you need an answer."

"In case you're still on the fence about going into business with me, I'm texting you some pics I took five seconds ago."

Glancing over at Bekah, Drew took in her baffled expression and smiled to reassure her. He angled the screen so they could both see and moved through another round of photos even prettier than the ones he'd seen earlier. "They're incredible, that's for sure. I'll call you tomorrow or the day after at the latest. 'Bye."

Once Drew hung up, he quickly filled her in on the opportunity he had to become a partner in Silver Creek Wilderness Adventures. When he was finished, Bekah stared at him in astonishment.

"What on earth are you doing, putting him off like that?" she demanded. "Being involved in something like this is your dream. Beyond that, you've always wanted to be your own boss. This is your chance."

"I know." Taking her hand, he absently rubbed the back of her knuckles before folding her fingers inside his. Meeting those beautiful eyes, he tried to explain what he was feeling. "It's just that I'm not sure it's a good time for me to leave."

"The farm work is winding down for winter," she pointed out in her practical way, "and donations are flooding into the rescue center. What's keeping you from flying to Colorado to check out Nolan's operation?"

"You." His short, simple answer got him a grateful smile. Bolstered by her reaction, he was inspired to ask, "Do you want to come with me?"

"Yes," she answered quickly, then frowned. "But I can't."

"I'll buy your ticket. There are all kinds of airfare deals right now if you don't mind traveling in the middle of the night."

"That's not the reason."

"Then what?" Hearing the near-whine in his voice, Drew steadied it before continuing, "I don't understand the problem."

"My family moved around constantly when I was

growing up, and after I left my parents' house, I kind of drifted around, looking for a place that felt like home." Pausing, she sat up a little straighter as if she was summoning the strength to forge ahead. "I found it here in Oaks Crossing, and at the clinic. Now that I have what I've been missing, I don't want to leave it behind for something I've never even seen that may or may not work out."

"So, come with me and see what you think," Drew all but begged, willing this very stubborn woman to agree. "No strings, I promise. I might hate it there, anyway."

"You won't," she predicted with unnerving confidence. "I saw your face when you were flipping through those pictures. You love the property already, and you haven't even seen it in person."

She had him there, Drew had to admit. He could only imagine the full effect of the mountains with a cool breeze blowing through and the wild sounds of the river and animals that must echo through the valleys full of trees. Even the early snowfall didn't faze him, which was really saying something for a guy who'd only seen it in movies.

Completely different from Kentucky, Colorado tugged at him with an almost physical force. Coupled with the idea of running a business that he would co-own only made the temptation harder to resist. "I haven't decided yet. I have to run it past my family first."

"Oh, please," she scoffed with a short laugh. "You know they'll tell you to go for it. It's not like you're moving out there tomorrow. You're just going to Denver to see your friend and get a tour. Then, if you like what you see, you can get more serious about making plans."

"You could do the same," he pointed out in a last-ditch attempt to convince her.

Very firmly, she shook her head. "I'm not going to give you some kind of false hope that I'm even the tiniest bit interested in going out there. But I do think you should go, because if you don't, you'll regret it someday. I refuse to be the one responsible for you giving up on your dream just when it could actually come true."

With that, she stood and kissed his cheek. Then, with a sad smile, she left him in his living room, watching her walk out his front door. He waited for her to look back, tell him she'd changed her mind, something. Even after she was gone, he stared out the front window for a few minutes, listening for footsteps on the gravel pathway telling him that she'd come back.

But she didn't.

Suddenly, he wasn't all that hungry anymore, so Drew slid the pan of lasagna into his nearly empty fridge, turned off the oven and wandered outside to think. Sitting on the porch steps, he stared into the woods beside the cottage, up at the old bead boards in the ceiling that needed a fresh coat of paint, down the road that led into town.

After about half an hour of debating the options with himself, he finally came to the conclusion that Bekah was right. If he didn't at least go to Denver and assess the layout for himself, he'd always be dogged by what-ifs.

So he grabbed a jacket and drove down the road to the farm. By a strange twist of fate, his entire family was there, gathered around the kitchen table in a scene he'd been part of for as long as he could recall.

Only this time, it was as if he was a stranger as he walked into his mother's kitchen. He'd never felt that way before, and it didn't sit well with him now. He couldn't help believing that it underscored the fact that his mind was already made up, and he was just going through the motions of considering the alternatives.

"There's my boy," Mom greeted him with a kiss and a bright smile. It quickly fell, though, and she asked, "What's wrong?"

"I have something to talk about with you. All of you." Settling on to the end of a bench, he sent a look around the table. "It's good, but I'm not sure what to do about it."

"You need pie," his mother announced, cutting a piece and piling on fresh whipped cream before sitting down in her armchair. "Go ahead."

Drew ignored the dessert while he filled his family in on this chance of a lifetime. They all asked him questions here and there, but mostly they listened.

Then, as usual, Mike got right down to the crux of the problem. "What do you want?"

"To be my own boss," Drew replied truthfully. "I enjoy working here with you and Josh, but I wouldn't mind having the room to find out what I could do on my own."

"You've earned it," Josh chimed in without the least bit of hesitation. "Ever since we were kids, you've always wanted to see other places. It sounds like this is the perfect situation for you."

"I started my own thing at the center," Erin added in an understanding tone. "And Mike and Josh have their specialties here at the farm. If this is your thing, then you should go after it. We're pretty resourceful—we'll figure out how to make it work here without you."

The others echoed her sentiment, but Mom was uncharacteristically quiet. Turning to her, Drew expected to find her mouth set in disapproval. Instead, to his amazement, she was beaming at him with pride. Reaching out a hand, she rested it on his as tears glistened in her eyes. "You've got so much of your father in you. I know if he was here with us now, he'd ask what on earth you're waiting for. Go home, pack a suitcase and get yourself to the airport."

Her comment was so similar to Bekah's, it threw him off his stride for a few seconds. "Really?" Glancing around the table again, he gave them one last opportunity to disagree. "You're all sure?"

"Just be sure to come back in time for Thanksgiving," Lily said, leaning over to kiss his cheek. "We'll all be waiting to see you."

"I will, promise." Heaving a relieved sigh, he smiled at the generous people seated around the old table. "Thanks, everyone. This means a lot to me."

Mike let out a mock growl. "Don't be getting all mushy on us. I'm still trying to eat."

They all laughed, and now that he was confident he had their full support, Drew's appetite returned with a vengeance. While he wolfed down his pie, Mom warmed up beef stew and her secret-recipe soda bread for him to eat.

So, the rest of his night was spent in the kitchen of the old farmhouse, surrounded by strong, loving people who had risen up to support him when he needed them the most. If his trip to Colorado proved to be the beginning of an exciting new adventure for him, he knew he'd never forget that without his family, it never would have happened.

The next morning, Bekah groaned when the crowing-rooster alarm on her phone went off. Not the best choice, she realized now, making a note to change it to something less jarring the first chance she got.

She hit the snooze and rolled onto her back, staring up at the rough-hewn beams in the ceiling with a sigh that came dangerously close to being a sob. She hadn't heard from Drew since leaving his house last night, but she assumed he was on his way to the airport to catch a flight that would take him to Colorado.

And away from her.

It wasn't fair, a bratty voice in her head insisted. Yesterday, she'd said goodbye to Rosie, and now she was losing Drew. Not long ago, she would have reminded herself that this was what you got when you allowed yourself to become too attached to anyone. But since she'd left her solitary existence behind and had opened herself up to caring about others, there was no choice but to accept the sad fact that she ran the risk of being disappointed by them.

To her surprise, that dark thought drifted through her mind very quickly and was replaced by a much brighter perspective. She'd done everything she could for Rosie, and the hawk had recovered to return to the life God intended her to have. And Drew...

All night long, she'd tossed and turned, trying to get him out of her head. Protective and sweet, early on the Kentucky farm boy had become someone she could depend on without worrying that he had some ulterior motive where she was concerned. Drew simply wanted what was best for her, a trait he'd demonstrated from the moment they met until last night when he'd gallantly tried to include her in the biggest decision of his life.

For his own sake, she'd left him alone to speak to his family and think through what would truly make him happy. Much as she wished that he would choose to stay in Oaks Crossing, she'd never do anything to rip his dream out of his grasp when it was so close to coming true. Remaining in his hometown might satisfy him for a while, but she feared that one day he'd regret sacrificing so much for her and end up hating her for it.

Losing the man she loved was heart-wrenching, but in time she'd adjust to life without him. Seeing his fondness for her erode and vanish would be more than she could bear.

Her alarm crowed again, and this time she dragged herself out of bed to get ready for her usual morning rounds. When she opened her door, she had to blink twice to believe her eyes.

There, sitting on the open tailgate of his truck, was Drew. A brightly checked tablecloth was spread over the tailgate, showcasing a delicious-looking assortment of Danish pastries and muffins that rivaled any continental breakfast she'd ever seen.

"Mornin'." Flashing one of those infernal grins, he took a sip from a mug of coffee steaming in the cool air.

"Morning." Completely bewildered, she slowly walked toward the truck while her foggy brain tried to compute what it was seeing.

"Hungry?" She hadn't eaten since lunch yesterday,

and her stomach growled a response loud enough to make him chuckle. "There's plenty. I wasn't sure what you'd like, so I got one of everything Cam had ready to go. Help yourself."

Still confused, she clambered onto the other end of the makeshift bench and picked up a blueberry muffin so moist, it fell apart in her hands. She popped a large piece into her mouth and hummed in appreciation. After she swallowed, she looked over at him, trying to get a sense of what was going on. Normally, she could read him fairly easily, but today his expression gave her no clue about what was going on behind those twinkling hazel eyes.

"Thank you for this," she said hesitantly, working up the courage to ask him the question that had been plaguing her for longer than she cared to admit. "Does this mean you've made a decision about Colorado?"

"Yeah, it does."

He seemed so pleased, she knew he'd finally gotten his wish. So, dredging up what she hoped was a reasonably happy look, she said, "That's wonderful, Drew. I know you'll be a huge success out there."

For some reason, he laughed. Shaking his head, he reached for her hand and held it snugly in his. "That may be, but I'm not going to Colorado."

Baffled by the unexpected revelation, she stared at him in amazement. "Why not? It's your dream to do something like that."

"Dreams change."

"I don't understand."

Reaching out, he cradled her cheek in his hand. Bringing her face to his, he brushed a tender kiss over her lips before smiling at her. "I love you, Bekah. That's why I'm staying."

This was too much, she thought with a smile of her own. Returning the kiss, she confided, "And I love you. That's why I told you to go."

"We're quite the pair, aren't we?"

"I think we make a pretty good team. I mean, when you're not getting in my way."

"Getting in your—" Stopping, he let out a long-suffering male sigh. "What have I gotten myself into?"

"I guess you'll have to stick around and find out."

"Well, if I'm gonna be doing that…" Reaching into the watch pocket of his jeans, he pulled out a lovely antique engagement ring. "I'm really hoping you'll make my new dream come true."

"Yes," she breathed without a tinge of doubt. The old Bekah couldn't have conceived of taking such a leap. But the woman she was now—the one Drew had discovered under all the tarnish—knew that marrying him was absolutely the right thing for her.

As he slid the ring onto her finger, she realized she wasn't shaking even the tiniest bit. She'd never experienced this kind of rock-solid certainty in her entire life, and feeling it now was so incredible she could hardly believe it.

Holding out her hand, she admired the setting that sparkled in spite of the dim morning light. Then it occurred to her how early it was, and she gave him a curious look. "How long have you had this?"

He extended his arm to check his nonexistent watch. "About half an hour. Why?"

"There's a jewelry store around here that's open at seven in the morning?"

210 Rescued by the Farmer

"There is when you know the owner."

"So you went into town, bought an engagement ring and then stopped at the café to buy breakfast?"

"Uh-huh."

All for her. Shaking her head, she asked, "Is there anything you won't do for me?"

"Not so far."

Delighted with the way things had turned out between them, she leaned in to kiss her everyday hero one more time. "I have to say, I really like your style."

Epilogue

"Got a minute?"

Glancing away from the standing mirror in his mother's bedroom, Drew settled the collar on his only suit jacket and chuckled. "Well, I'm kinda busy marrying Bekah and all. What'd you need?"

In reply, Mike held out a large, thick envelope for him. Curious about what was going on, Drew tore into it and pulled out a sheaf of oversize legal papers. A quick scan of the cover page told him the basics, and he stared at his brother in disbelief. "You're giving me the buffer zone behind the farm?"

"I had it surveyed, and there's fifty-six acres back there, with plenty of standing timber and the best part of the creek. I figure if you clear some of the trees out, you can start your own wilderness tourism business and still be close by if things get crazy around here."

"Mike, I don't know what to say." Tossing the papers on to a chair, he gave his brother a grateful hug. "This is the best wedding present ever. Thank you."

"You're welcome. And before you ask—no, it wasn't

Lily's idea to do this. She agreed that it was a good gift, though."

"It's perfect. Did everyone else know about it?"

"Are you kidding?" Mike scoffed. "No one in this family can keep a secret beyond the kitchen door. I figured that once you get the site ready, Bekah can help you out with your website and advertising. She seems to have a knack for that technical stuff."

Drew couldn't keep back a grin. "Among other things."

Mike rolled his eyes, and Drew was laughing when Josh poked his head in. "Pastor Wheaton's here."

"Awesome." Drew clapped his hands together eagerly. "I'm ready."

"You sure?" Josh asked.

Slinging an arm around his shoulders, Drew herded him into the hallway. "Little brother, when you find the right woman, you're always sure."

Josh glanced at Mike, who simply nodded. Then the youngest Kinley shook his head in bewilderment as he continued down the hallway to Mike and Lily's room, which was serving as the girls' dressing area. "Whatever. I'll go get Bekah and meet you guys downstairs."

Early December was too chilly for the outdoor ceremony they would have preferred, but when Drew saw how the women of the family had decorated the farmhouse's front parlor, he couldn't imagine how the setting could be any prettier.

Greenery dotted with lilies and roses was draped along the ceiling and around the tall windows and doors, tied in place with enormous white ribbons. He recognized the white runner on the floor from Mike's wedding carriage business, and the collection of mismatched chairs for their guests had come from the Kinleys' various homes.

His entire family had come together to give Bekah the wedding she deserved. He only prayed they knew how much their efforts meant to her.

"This is fantastic," he said to his best man. "It looks like the girls dragged the whole garden in here."

"They're Kinleys," Mike reminded him with a chuckle. "When they set their mind to something, there's no stopping them."

A few minutes later, Mrs. Wheaton pressed some buttons on her electric keyboard and switched from muted classical music to the famous march that Drew had begun to think he'd never hear played for his own wedding. The guests all stood, and he followed their gazes to the flower-accented archway.

Abby skipped in, sprinkling flower petals while Parker carefully balanced their wedding rings on a small pillow. Behind them, Erin, Lily and Sierra walked forward and formed a pretty line on the bride's side of the room.

And then, Josh appeared in the foyer with Bekah on his arm. Drew vaguely registered that she was wearing a lacy white dress and carrying a bouquet, but as she came toward him, all he saw was the beautiful smile on her face. At the end of the short aisle, Josh stooped to kiss her cheek and somberly pass her delicate hand over to Drew before stepping back to take his seat.

"Morning, sunshine," he whispered as she settled in beside him. Now that he'd gotten past his initial stunning, he gave her a quick once-over. "Nice dress. Is it new?"

She laughed out loud, and out of the corner of his

eye he saw Mom look up, as if to complain about him to Dad the way she used to. The gesture reminded him of when Bekah had commented on how they all talked about their father so much, it was as if he was still around. With the whole family gathered for such a happy occasion, Drew had no trouble believing that Justin Kinley was looking down on them, enjoying the day.

The music trailed off into silence, and the pastor greeted everyone before opening his Bible to begin the simple ceremony Drew and Bekah had chosen. To Drew, it felt like the familiar verses spoken at so many weddings flew by in a single heartbeat.

Before he realized it, he heard himself repeating the vows he'd once thought he'd never say, ending with, "With this ring, I thee wed."

As he slid the polished gold band onto Bekah's finger, she gazed up at him with joy lighting her eyes. Then she repeated her vows and gave him the ring she'd bought for him. It was different from hers, but he didn't have a chance to look more closely as the preacher said, "And now, I present to you, Mr. and Mrs. Andrew Kinley."

After they'd run the gauntlet of well-wishing guests and found some breathing room out on the front porch, Drew took a moment to admire the circle of branches and leaves carved into the gold. "This is really cool. Where'd you find it?"

"A friend of mine in Maryland makes custom jewelry. When I told her you were an outdoorsy kind of guy, she sketched this design for me, and I thought it was perfect. I'm glad you like it."

"Very much." Folding her hand in his, he kissed

the rings sparkling there. Then he noticed her eyes were sparkling even brighter, and he chuckled. "You know about the wedding gift Mike and Lily gave us, don't you?"

"Lily told me about it upstairs. She figured it was okay to spill the beans, because by the time we saw each other, you'd already know. What a generous, thoughtful thing for Mike to do."

"Keep in mind, that acreage hasn't been touched since my grandfather bought it from the farmer behind us sixty years ago. It's full of rotting tree branches, brambles and several different kinds of snakes."

"Sounds like a great spot for you."

Her saucy look made him laugh. "Yeah, it does. Once I get a space cleared out for paying guests to camp in, anyway."

"If you need an extra set of hands, I'm pretty good with an ax."

"Get out," he scoffed. "A cute little thing like you—how'd that happen?"

Laughing, she draped her wrists over his shoulders and gave him a playful kiss. "Now that we're married, you'll find that I'm just full of surprises."

"Yeah?" he replied, drawing her in for another kiss. "I'm looking forward to that."

* * * * *

If you loved this story,
pick up the first OAKS CROSSING *book,*
HER SMALL-TOWN COWBOY,
and these other stories of small-town life
from author Mia Ross's previous miniseries
BARRETT'S MILL:

BLUE RIDGE REUNION
SUGAR PLUM SEASON
FINDING HIS WAY HOME
LOVING THE COUNTRY BOY

Available now from Love Inspired!

Find more great reads at www.Harlequin.com.

Dear Reader,

I hope you enjoyed your visit to Oaks Crossing!

The opening scene of this book was inspired by my own near-miss with a dive-bombing hawk who was more intent on snagging his breakfast than avoiding my car. After my heart rate settled back down, I realized that I'd been more concerned about him being injured (or worse) than I was about the potential damage to my windshield. From there, Bekah Holloway's life-altering encounter with Rosie and the other residents of the Oaks Crossing Rescue Center took shape. Because the animals weren't the only ones in need of saving, the story became one about confronting a difficult past, putting it to rest and moving on to a bright new future.

Getting to know Bekah was fascinating, but learning about Drew proved to be just as interesting. There was more to the charming, easygoing middle Kinley brother than met the eye, and as Bekah's fondness for him grew, so did mine. Putting aside his own dreams to stay in Oaks Crossing and support his family showed a lot of character, and his willingness to give Bekah the help she so desperately needed made him just what she calls him: an everyday hero.

He's the type of person who steps up day in and day out, doing what they can to make their slice of the world a nicer place. They're the teachers who stay longer at school to give our kids some one-on-one time, or a neighbor who notices that our driveway is buried in snow and drives his plow over to help us clear it out. Sometimes, they take their tractor down to mow an overgrown playground not because they'll get paid to do it, but because they want kids to enjoy the park.

Those are my kind of people, and my real-life small town is full of them. I sincerely hope you know a few of them, too, because they make life better for all of us.

If you'd like to stop by for a visit, you'll find me online at www.miaross.com, Facebook, Twitter, Goodreads and Pinterest. When you get a chance, send me a message in your favorite format. I'd love to hear from you!

Mia Ross

COMING NEXT MONTH FROM
Love Inspired®

Available July 19, 2016

A BEAU FOR KATIE
The Amish Matchmaker • by Emma Miller

An accident leaves Freeman Kemp with a broken leg—and no choice but to find a housekeeper. He never imagines that hiring Katie Byler will turn his household—and his heart—upside down.

THE TEXAN'S SECOND CHANCE
Blue Thorn Ranch • by Allie Pleiter

Determined to overcome his black-sheep reputation, Witt Buckton takes command of Blue Thorn Ranch's new food-truck business. Hiring the talented Jana Powers as head chef will bring him one step closer to success—and to love.

HER UNEXPECTED FAMILY
Grace Haven • by Ruth Logan Herne

Single dad Grant McCarthy is all about family—even taking on planning his sister's wedding while she's deployed overseas. As he falls for wedding planner Emily Gallagher, can he also make room in his life for a wife?

THE BACHELOR'S SWEETHEART
The Donnelly Brothers • by Jean C. Gordon

They've always been just friends, but when Josh Donnelly and Tessa Hamilton team up to renovate her movie theater, their feelings deepen. Will their blossoming romance survive after Tessa reveals a dark secret she's kept hidden?

SMALL-TOWN GIRL
Goose Harbor • by Jessica Keller

Starting over in Goose Harbor, Kendall Mayes opens her dream business, which brings her into contact with handsome loner Brice Daniels. But everything could fall apart if he discovers her secret business partner is the man he hates most.

LAKESIDE ROMANCE
by Lisa Jordan

Sarah Sullivan's new life plan involves making a success of her church's summer community outreach program—and excludes love. Until she asks Alec Seaver to help teach her charges how to cook—and begins to reconsider a future that includes her handsome neighbor.

LOOK FOR THESE AND OTHER LOVE INSPIRED BOOKS WHEREVER BOOKS ARE SOLD, INCLUDING MOST BOOKSTORES, SUPERMARKETS, DISCOUNT STORES AND DRUGSTORES.

LICNM0716

REQUEST YOUR FREE BOOKS!

2 FREE INSPIRATIONAL NOVELS
PLUS 2
FREE
MYSTERY GIFTS

Love Inspired®

SPECIAL EXCERPT FROM

Love Inspired®

When a handsome Amish mill owner breaks his leg, a feisty young Amish woman agrees to be his housekeeper. But will two weeks together lead to romance or heartbreak?

Read on for a sneak preview of
A BEAU FOR KATIE,
the third book in Emma Miller's miniseries
THE AMISH MATCHMAKER.

"Here's Katie," Sara the matchmaker announced. "She'll lend a hand with the housework until you're back on your feet." She motioned Katie to approach the bed. "I think you two already know each other."

"*Ya*," Freeman admitted gruffly. "We do."

Katie removed her black bonnet. Freeman Kemp wasn't hard on the eyes. Even lying flat in a bed, one leg in a cast, he was still a striking figure of a man. The pain lines at the corners of his mouth couldn't hide his masculine jaw. His wavy brown hair badly needed a haircut, and he had at least a week's growth of dark beard, but the cotton undershirt revealed broad, muscular shoulders and arms.

Freeman's compelling gaze met hers. His eyes were brown, almost amber, with darker swirls of color. Unnerved, she uttered in a hushed tone, "Good morning, Freeman."

Then Katie turned away to inspect the kitchen that would be her domain for the next two weeks. She'd never been inside the house before, but from the outside, she'd thought it was beautiful. Now, standing in the spacious kitchen, she liked it even more. The only thing that looked out of place was the bed containing the frowning Freeman.

"You must be in a lot of pain," Sara remarked, gently patting Freeman's cast.

"*Ne*. Nothing to speak of."

Katie nodded. "Well, rest and proper food for an invalid will do you the most good."

Freeman glanced away. "I'm *not* an invalid."

Katie sighed. If your leg encased in a cast didn't make you an invalid, she didn't know what did. But Freeman, as she recalled, had a stubborn nature.

For an eligible bachelor who owned a house, a mill and two hundred acres of prime land to remain single into his midthirties was almost unheard of among the Amish. Add to that, Freeman's rugged good looks. It made him the catch of the county. They could have him. She was not a giggling teenager who could be swept off her feet by a pretty face. Working in his house for two whole weeks wasn't going to be easy, but he didn't intimidate her. She'd told Sara she'd take the job and she was a woman of her word.

Don't miss
A BEAU FOR KATIE by Emma Miller,
available August 2016 wherever
Love Inspired® books and ebooks are sold.

www.LoveInspired.com

With her uncle trying to claim her ranch, widow
Lula May Barlow has no time to worry about romance.
But can she resist Edmund McKay—the handsome
cowboy next door—when he helps her fight for her
land…and when her children start playing matchmaker?

Read on for a sneak preview of
A FAMILY FOR THE RANCHER,
the heartwarming continuation of the series
LONE STAR COWBOY LEAGUE:
THE FOUNDING YEARS

"Just wanted to return your book."

Book?

Lula May saw her children slinking out of the barn, guilty looks on their faces. So that's why they'd made such nuisances of themselves out at the pasture. They'd wanted her to send them off to play so they could take the book to Edmund. And she knew exactly why. Those little rascals were full-out matchmaking! Casting a look at Edmund, she faced the inevitable, which wasn't really all that bad. "Will you come in for coffee?"

He tilted his hat back to reveal his broad forehead, where dark blond curls clustered and made him look younger than his thirty-three years. "Coffee would be good."

Lula May led him in through the back door. To her horror, Uncle sat at the kitchen table hungrily eyeing the cake she'd made for Edmund…and almost forgotten about. Now she'd have no excuse for not introducing them before she figured out how to get rid of Floyd.

"Edmund, this is Floyd Jones." She forced herself to add, "My uncle. Floyd, this is my neighbor, Edmund McKay."

As the children had noted last week when Edmund first

stepped into her kitchen, he took up a good portion of the room. Even Uncle seemed a bit unsettled by his presence. While the men chatted about the weather, however, Lula May could see the old wiliness and false charm creeping into Uncle's words and facial expressions. She recognized the old man's attempt to figure Edmund out so he could control him.

Pauline and Daniel worked at the sink, urgent whispers going back and forth. Why had they become so bold in their matchmaking? Was it possible they sensed the danger of Uncle's presence and wanted to lure Edmund over here to protect her? She wouldn't have any of that. She'd find a solution without any help from anybody, especially not her neighbor. Her only regret was that she hadn't been able to protect the children from realizing Uncle wasn't a good man. If she could have found a way to be nicer to him… No, that wasn't possible. Not when he'd come here for the distinct purpose of seizing everything she owned.

The men enjoyed their coffee and cake, after which Edmund suggested they take a walk around the property to build up an appetite for supper.

"We'd like to go for a walk with you, Mr. McKay," Pauline said. "May we, Mama?"

Lula May hesitated. Let them continue their matchmaking or make them spend time with Uncle? Neither option pleased her. When had she lost control of her household? About a week before Uncle arrived, that was when, the day when Edmund had walked into her kitchen and invited himself into her…or rather, her eldest son's life.

"You may go, but don't pester Mr. McKay." She gave the children a narrow-eyed look of warning.

Their innocent blinks did nothing to reassure her.

Don't miss
A FAMILY FOR THE RANCHER
by Louise M. Gouge, available August 2016 wherever
Love Inspired® *Historical books and ebooks are sold.*

www.LoveInspired.com